Song for Eloise

Song for Eloise

Leigh Sauerwein

BLOOMSBURY

Merci Béatrice et Eric

Thank you, Stephen

First published in Great Britain in 2006 by Bloomsbury Publishing Plc,
36 Soho Square, London W1D 3QY

First published in America in 2003 by Front Street Books
862 Haywood Road, Asheville,
North Carolina, NC 28806

A CIP catalogue record of this book is available from the British Library

ISBN 0 7475 7813 3
ISBN 9780747578130

Printed in Great Britain by Clays Ltd, St Ives Plc

1 3 5 7 9 10 8 6 4 2

All papers used by Bloomsbury Publishing are natural, recyclable products
made from wood grown in well-managed forests. The manufacturing processes
conform to the environmental regulations of the country of origin.

Escoutatz!
E non sap vas qual part fuja
cel qui del foc es gastatz!

Listen!
He who is devoured by the fire
will not know where to run!

IN THOSE DAYS SHE WOULD HANG FROM HER FATHER'S neck like a little monkey, and he would laugh his rumbling laugh and turn around and around in the big room, and her feet would fly out but she would never fall. Those were the winter months, when he hardly ever rode away to war or to tournaments, the months when he stayed at home. The fires seemed to burn more brightly then, her mother's face lost its fierce contours, and the orders to the house servants were given in gentler tones.

She and her brothers and sisters always knew when they could "climb the mountain," the name they gave to the game of hanging from their father's shoulders and arms. They could always tell from the set of his mouth and a certain expression in his eyes that the time was right, that he was feigning his indifference and waiting for their assault. Giggling and whispering from the shadows behind him as he sat before the fire in his high-backed chair, they would crawl along the floor, all five of them, until Arnaud, the oldest, would stand and shout the battle cry, "On to him! On to him!" And they would jump up, screaming and leaping forward, whereupon he would growl like a bear and pretend great fury and lurch to his feet as they flung themselves at him. And then he would stagger and groan his way around the room with them hanging from all sides and roar away until they all fell down laughing.

Only she, Eloise, would not let go, would not drop to the floor with the others. She was always the last, so light, clinging so tightly that he would have to unhook her arms and set her down. Always the first to say to the others, "Let's begin again." And the five of them would retreat behind the heavy curtain that led into the room, keep silent for a few seconds, and then get down on their hands and knees to begin another approach while their parents went on speaking quietly before the fire, pretending not to notice.

"ELOISE, YOU LEECH," HER FATHER WOULD RASP IN her ear when the game ended, but she alone could stay on after the others had been sent off to bed, she alone was allowed to fall asleep in his lap, her ear pressed against his chest listening to his heart beat and his voice rumble as she drifted off. Perhaps he allowed this because she was the youngest of the five, perhaps because he knew there would be no more children after her, that she was his last.

After a time, her mother would lift her up and she would leave the leathery father smell for the lavender mother smell, and be carried away as if on a river in a drifting boat, down and around, down and around the winding stone stairs, past the oil lamps burning in their alcoves, all the way to the wide bed she shared with her sisters. And there she would sink into sleep again, just her little shoes pulled off and slipped onto the floor because it was so far into the night and her mother did not want to disturb the others.

The night hours begin when the sun goes down, the day hours begin when it rises. With the changing seasons, the length of the nights and the days changes constantly. On a monk's writing table, the sand is running down through an hourglass.

In March, the night is twelve hours long, the day twelve.
In April, the night is ten hours long, the day fourteen.

HER HAIR WAS STILL BLOND IN THOSE DAYS, HAD NOT yet darkened and thickened into the wild curls she would have later. Oh, the tugging, tugging of the comb

11

as she sat in the sunshine between her mother's knees and the pressure of her mother's fingers on her head, feeling for lice and rubbing vinegar into her scalp to keep them away. And then to the steam room, plunging her into a barrel of warm water, scrubbing her from head to toe, the cloth foaming from the cake of soap. "A bath is like a good confession," her mother inevitably said at one point during the washing. "It leaves you feeling light and pure."

Today those short years in her father's castle seemed to be turning into a dream. Had she really once looked up into the fierce blue eyes so like her own, into that face framed by a reddish beard flecked with grey? Had she really once listened to that rumbling, laughing growl and felt the scratchy softness of those kisses on her cheek? And been carried to a large bed in her mother's arms and laid to sleep next to Hedwige and Eleanor, her sisters?

Had she once trailed and stumbled after Bertrand and Arnaud, her older brothers, as they ran along the riverbank with their sharp sticks and their battle plans?

"Let me come too!" she had shouted. "I want to go with you!" But her brothers had only laughed and run faster, leaving her far behind. Leaving her to Flora, the house girl, a plump creature scarcely older than she, who had come running down huffing and puffing to yank her up and drag her to her mother, who waited with a green switch for her bare legs. And later, when they left her altogether, left her able only to watch them as they began their training to become men. Watching from a narrow window, the two of them, tall Arnaud and stocky Bertrand, as they mounted up and rode out into the world. For a day, for a week, for a month, under wind and rain, through forest and field, unattached as yet to any house and belonging only to God. Then entering service and gone for years. Then gone altogether, on the crusade, never to come riding back to the home towers again. And her father's spirit broken by his grief.

Eloise feels her mother's hands on her own, firm, molding them like clay to her will, showing her how to push the needle down in one place and then up again a tiny distance away, how to make the stitches turn into a pattern, how to create a field of flowers with the many-coloured tiny beads, or a leopard's shining eye. And she hears the murmuring women's voices as they all worked at their spinning and sewing and embroidery, she hears the whirring of the spinning wheel and the talking as it turned into singing and then back into talking again. A song comes to her, that round from up north. Once all the voices had chimed in, it sounded like bells ringing: *Orléans, Beaugency, Notre Dame de Cléry, Vendôme.* All through the afternoons until the fading of the light.

THE WAGON RATTLES IN HER EARS, BUMPING AND shaking her from side to side. She grips at the railing, hangs on more tightly. There is a stain of berries on her white dress. Her legs hurt, and up between her legs there is a different pain and perhaps, she thinks, some blood. The railing trembles under her fingers. The flowers in her hair have begun to droop and wilt. The night is warm. Across from her, Flora is snivelling, rolled up in a ball on her cushion like a fat dog. Eloise pulls the crown of flowers down out of her hair. Flora stifles a sob. "Oh, shut up, will you!" Eloise snaps at her. Flora sniffs and falls silent.

The wagon continues to tremble and shake as it lurches up the steep mountain road between towering trees and jutting boulders. Eloise is thrown back against the wooden seat. She hears the horses straining, the harness leather creaking, the driver whipping at the animals with a long branch of green.

Somewhere ahead rides a man named Robert. "My husband," Eloise says to herself, but the words sound empty. The rattling wagon is covered with white ribbons. Eloise can barely see them in the dark. She can smell the petals from the flowers under her feet, a sweet faintly rotting fragrance, and also a sharper smell from the blue-green pine boughs tied to the sides of the wagon. Some of Robert's men have begun to sing. She cannot make out the words, but the song has a lilting rhythm and the men laugh when they have finished. And after a time they begin another one. Eloise takes off her shoes and pushes her toes down into the petals. She is married. She is a lady.

"YOU ARE TO MARRY ROBERT, MARRY ROBERT, MARRY Robert ..." The words had rung in her ears. At first, looking at her father and her mother, she had wondered if she had heard them correctly. And since she was accustomed to speaking freely, she had laughed and exclaimed, "What, that black-bearded old grump? That bear? Not Robert of Rochefort? That rude, that gross—"

"Hold your tongue, girl, keep still!" Her father had never shouted at her, she had never heard such a tone in his voice. In an instant he had changed, no longer her father, but Baudoin the sword wielder, a lord, a holder of land, master of the river and the river fortresses, of village and forest and field three days' riding in any direction, as far as the eye could see. The kings of France and Aragon were strong, but in that mountainous middle land it was Baudoin who said what was right and wrong, Baudoin who decided what was to be done.

"Robert has all my trust," her father had said then. "He is a man of great courage and my faithful friend. You will find him in time to be kind. He is not yet old and his heart is good."

"And that good heart will live in your children," came her mother's voice, firm, reassuring.

"I will hear no more talk from you," her father had added quietly. And the great grief for her brothers that she could hear behind his words kept her head bowed and her tongue silent.

She had turned away from them then and stared at the oil lamp hanging from the ceiling on its four chains, each fastened to the head of a dragon whose bodies came together in a hollow where the flame flickered from side to side, licking out at the edges of the blackened bowl. She felt her heart sinking like a stone just thrown into the river.

It is pruning time in the vineyards. The men who work there are sharpening their hooked blades.

In March, the night is twelve hours long, the day twelve.
In April, the night is ten hours long, the day fourteen.

THERE HAD INDEED BEEN NO MORE TALK AFTER THAT. And before she knew it, everything had been planned. Robert would come down from the mountain fortress at Eastertime.

"Fifteen summers she, and thirty winters he," went the ditty the castle people began to chant before the wedding, around the bread oven and the well. *"Once her beauty he has seen, she will make his winter green ..."* And soon the song sounded from the fields and from the river too, from the kitchens and from under the ringing of the black-smith's hammer. It seemed to be everywhere.

And then quickly, too quickly, the weeks flying past as if at a gallop, the wedding day came.

A house servant has tipped his pitcher, and a small stream of oil is filling the hollow of a lamp.

Horses are jostling each other in a stable.

A peasant woman slides her bare feet into a pair of wooden clogs. She clip-clops down a muddy road to the vineyards.

BEFORE SUNRISE ON HER WEDDING DAY, ELOISE HAD slipped out of the bed without waking her sisters and crept up stairways and ladders all the way to the top of the castle. She had lain down for a while on the flat stones and watched the stars begin to dim. Today the maids would lower the satin dress embroidered with twenty pearls over her lifted arms and then they would fasten the crown of flowers into her hair. Down below she heard Thomas, the oven boy, come to light the fire, as he did every day before dawn. She heard him whistling and then the familiar creak of the oven door as he swung it open. And the crackle of the twigs, the thump of the logs as he pushed them in, then the steady hum of the flames. He had stopped whistling and begun a song in his clear voice:

> *To ask your way,*
> *if this you know,*
> *through all the world,*
> *your steps may go.*

She had repeated the words, moving her lips without a sound. She heard him leaving, whistling again, but the familiar sound became fainter and fainter until it was gone.

THEN, SUDDENLY, SHE WAS WITH ROBERT, STANDING beside him in the church, and he had seemed even more silent and grim than she remembered. Her dress was heavy, both soft and scratchy, her unruly hair neatly combed, hanging down her back and crowned with a double ring of green tendrils and white blossoms. And when her father had stepped forward,

almost pushing Father Bernard off-balance, in order
to pull their hands together himself, it was as if he were
saying to the priest, You may bless, but I decide.

The instant her fingers touched Robert's, she could
tell that he was trembling. This gruff Robert, this
horseman, this sword wielder, this man of war, her
father's great friend, his hands were shaking like leaves
under the wind. And she had thought without showing
anything on her face, Well, so this is a man.

It was almost morning when she and he were
thrown together. The revellers from the wedding feast
had danced them along the riverbank to the wooden
wedding house wreathed with garlands and leaves. The
servants had dragged the wide bed down the day before
and laid in the mattress of fine wool, the linen sheets,
and the damask covers her uncle John had brought
back from Jerusalem when she was a little girl. And
old Bernard had blessed the bed and slipped a bouquet
of rosemary under her pillow.

Flora and another house girl held a long silken
sheet up in the middle of the room while her mother
and sisters lifted off her dress and slipped a soft, light
shift over her head. On the other side of the shimmering cloth, Robert's companions were dressing him
in a similar long shirt. All the while men's and
women's voices mingled in song from both sides of

the makeshift curtain. Then there were repeated countings of "One, two, three!" and "Are you ready?" and "No, not yet, she is not ready!" and finally a last, loud "One, two, three" and the cover was thrown into the air and all ran out of the little house, leaving the two of them face to face. One of the young men gave Robert a push forward before rushing out the door and slamming it shut. Robert staggered slightly, then regained his balance.

They stared at each other. Her hair was wild again, her cheeks were flushed. She sat down on the bed, feeling dizzy. They could still hear chanting and giggling outside. There were a few knocks on the walls, a few shrieks, and someone made kissing noises. But the merrymakers went away after that. Robert came and sat down beside her on the bed. He stared down into his hands, pulling at his fingers.

"I have always thought of you," he said after a time, raising his head and staring straight forward. "Always. Ever since I first saw you when you were a little girl. When you used to run after your brothers, along the riverbank." He turned toward her then and she met his gaze. "There has never been another in my thoughts."

Looking into Robert's eyes, Eloise saw his awe of her give way to determination.

WHEN THE SUN CAME UP ON THE MORNING AFTER THE wedding, Thomas was walking toward the river. He had fired the oven, as he did every day before going to work with his father, a fisherman. He walked through the faint light, and as usual the rhythm of his walking brought the singing words back into his head. He fingered the reed flute in his pocket. The first time he heard a trobar's song, he was only a boy, hanging back with the kitchen people before he had dared to begin creeping into the great hall, inching forward until he could see the lady Agnes at the high table beside her husband, the tall, red-bearded lord, and a bright blond head that seemed always to be dancing around them, never sitting still like the other children, her brothers and sisters. Little Eloise. There had come a pause in the eating and Baudoin had made a sign to a man who had risen from the foot of the table and come forward and begun to sing. The words had spoken of joy, but they had brought a strange pain into Thomas's heart. Taking in the singing words, he had felt his heart soar as if in prayer, and yet, at the same time, tears had come welling up in his eyes.

In that song, the likes of which he had never heard, the trobar had sung of his love for a lady, such a love that it made winter cold seem to turn into flowers and the white snow into leaves of green:

E la neus verdura.
And the snow, leaves of green.

ROBERT'S BREATH CAME FAST AT HER NECK AND SHE grasped at his back and tried to move in the way this thing should be done. Suddenly she remembered the hillside where she and her brothers had watched and shouted during the summer games, crunching blades of grass between their teeth, digging their nails into the earth, pounding the ground with their toes.

Where is father? Where is the blue banner? There! There he goes! And the two war horses would surge forward, thundering toward each other.

"Our house! Our house!" they would shout in their high voices. And then the thud and clash of impact would sound in their ears. "Red is down! We got him! We win! And now who comes? The white, look, the black and white one! Oh that's only Peire of Brioude. Father will take him easily." And again she and her brothers would wait for the jolting forward of the horses, the men as one with their mounts, shields raised, lances lifting, and again the thud and the crash and the shouting from the crowds in the stands and from the top of the castle walls and then, above all, the dizzying rush, feet pounding downhill over the grass to see their triumphant father pulling off his helmet ringed with chain mail, forehead sweaty and bleeding a little over one brow, to see his shining eyes and his smile and hear him exclaim, "My little wolves! My leech! What?! Not with your mother?" And she would shriek with glee, "No! No! No!"

But he would not scold them, only laugh and ride away to his men.

She had moved in the right way, she thought. Now she felt some pain but it was not too bad. This grim Robert slept, and she knew that it was she who had brought him this particular deep sleep. His face in repose was less forbidding. His beard was indeed very black, but not so ugly, she decided. She laid her head down on the pillow next to him. But sleep eluded her. She slid her hand under the pillow, reaching for the rosemary. She pressed the soft pointed leaves against her mouth and nose, closing her eyes and breathing. In the garden of earthly paradise she knew there were lilies and daisies and strawberries, shiny bright. She tried to think of them, tried to see the fruit and the flowers and the four rivers that flowed there from a fountain, four enchanted rivers flowing north and south, east and west, and gradually growing so wide that they carried ships between their greening banks.

Playing under the big table, she would sit on her mother's feet, grabbing at the dogs, and sometimes, on the quieter evenings, she would roll her fingers into a ball and knock on the wooden roof over her head and then wait for her father to say in his most courtly tones, "My dear lady Agnes, we have a visitor. Who could it be, I wonder?"

She thought of the dogs, how she liked to watch them wolf down the bits of bread soaked in the cooking juices that the guests would throw to them as they finished the meats. She thought of the maids in the kitchen during the afternoons when they plucked the chickens, how they held the limp, lifeless bodies across their aproned laps, pulling out the feathers by handfuls and tossing them into a wooden basin on the floor, and how some of the feathers would float around in the air before settling slowly as if snow had fallen carelessly here and there. And up in the old room with her sisters, how they used to laugh together, clothes scattered across the bed, clothes strewn this way and that, nothing folded and in place. And the sunlight in that same room, just a few days ago, sunlight falling on a red damask covering, on blue silk, on white linen. Packing the big trunk with her mother, folding her dresses and laying them in, one on top of the other, putting in her shoes, each pair joined with a leather cord, and then the jewels that were hers, her bracelets, her silver belts going into a sculpted wooden casket with a bronze lock. She stifled a sob. Sleep would not come.

She heard Arnaud shouting out of the past, "John is home! John is home!" and the rare sound of her mother's laughter. Her uncle John, her father's youngest brother. Back from his pilgrimage after three years' absence, his skin burned from the sun of those lands. His cheeks, his hands, even his feet. "See the marks of my sandals?" he had said to them all before the autumn fireplace, showing his bare feet still faintly marked by the sun. "It is so hot that you can wear nothing else," he said. "Our own shoes are impossible." She had hung back, grasping her mother's sleeve, made shy suddenly by this lean young man whom she scarcely remembered and who looked so strange with his dark face and shining eyes as he told his stories of the land where the lord Jesus had walked up and down. The places where the lord Jesus walked, John had walked there too, and he had touched those places with his hands, he had kissed that ground and he had also kissed the stone of the Holy Sepulchre where the lord Jesus rose up into paradise and he had returned safe and sound from over the big sea to tell about all these things. He had gone, back in those days, not as a man of arms but as a pilgrim. Not to fight but to see and learn and pray. She had lain curled up in her mother's lap listening to John talk on and on. "We passed the island of Sicily, where a great volcano belches fire and molten lava into the air. You would think," he said slowly, measuring the power of his words, "you would think you were looking at the very mouth of hell."

It was late. She had drifted off, awakened again, and still John was telling of his travels. "I stood in the river," he was saying, "where the Holy Ghost came down in the form of a dove, where our Lord was baptised, and I lay back and let the water roll over me." She slept and woke, slept and woke, and after a time the fire mountain and the dove flying down from heaven got all mixed up in her mind with the tale of the sea voyage and how the flying fish soared through the air and how once a pair of migrating birds fell exhausted onto the deck of the surging ship.

When she had opened her eyes the next morning in the bed with her sisters she had felt something lodged under her pillow. Reaching, she had pulled out two fat little cloth birds embroidered in blue and red. They had shining black eyes and seemed to be tightly stuffed with a perfumed powder of some kind. Later that day her mother had hung them carefully over a silver plate from a slender cord and showed her how to pierce their breasts with a needle. With each piercing, a tiny stream of powder would sift down onto the plate and sweeten the air in the room.

"John got them for you on the island called Cyprus where he lived for almost a year," her mother had said. And all through the year after John's return she had treasured the birds and some days she would squeeze them gently to make more powder come.

On summer mornings, rising before dawn, hunched at the narrow window and looking out at the dark, she would flick the birds with one fingertip to make them swing back and forth and smell them up close when they bumped at her nose while she waited for the fire boy. It was fun to whistle at him from her high window and make him start and turn around and wonder where the sound could be coming from at such an early hour. She would laugh to herself as she watched him look around. It was a good game. She was safe back then when she had slept in the bed with her older sisters, her mother's evening voice nearby, praying over them and lulling them to sleep, her prayer voice endlessly reciting in that singsong way, making them curl up into themselves, safe for sleep and safe from hunger and harm, all rolled together behind the stone walls under the blankets that smelled of lavender and thyme.

Now it was the smell of rosemary that lingered on her skin. She kept her hand up against her face and watched the man who lay asleep beside her.

As Eloise fell into sleep at last beside her new husband, Thomas worked with his father, the sun already high, their boats side by side in the stream with the net down between them. They began a new hauling up and the river fish with their silvery sides tumbled and flipped out onto the wooden deck. As Thomas pulled at the heavy net, hand over hand, he wondered, could not help wondering, if she lay now beside the baron Robert, and what she looked like as she slept. Soon they would be leaving, and she would climb up into the wagon all covered with flowers and pine boughs and be driven away, out of the valley and into the mountains. His thoughts flew back unbidden to a whistling sound from somewhere up high behind him, a little whistling sound coming out of the dark.

The rattling has stopped, the wagon has come to a halt. The wedding party has reached the mountain fortress, its destination. This new courtyard is small. Eloise rises to her feet. She has forgotten to put her shoes back on and she steps down barefoot onto the cold stones. She feels the blood between her legs. Robert.

Her mother had hung the wedding sheet from a window so all could see the stain. She hears him shouting to his men as they dismount. The horses' hooves clatter and thump. The crown of tendrils and flowers hangs from her fingers, and her braids have come loose.

Suddenly a tall woman with black hair emerges from the shadows, walking toward her with sure and even steps. Now they are standing face to face. The older woman seems to be examining her, appraising her without a word of greeting. Instinctively Eloise raises her chin, and her eyes go cold to meet the dark gaze. She, the daughter of Baudoin and the lady Agnes, will not be looked at in this way. The woman steps forward and, extending one hand, caresses the girl's cheek without a smile. Then quickly reaches out and places both hands on her breasts, squeezing slightly, then moving down, feeling her belly, her hips, for all the world as if she were a horse. A smile comes to the woman's face. "Very beautiful, very good," she says in a voice that is deep for a woman. "I am Lady Merle, Robert's mother." She reaches up and touches the young girl's face again, her forehead, the tip of her nose, her hair. "Welcome to the mountain," she says.

Eloise thanks her coldly, swearing to put a ring of maids between herself and this disrespectful blackbird. "Flora!" she almost shouts.

"Will you take my arm?" comes the soft, low voice once again. And suddenly with a shock Eloise knows that the dark eyes cannot see. "Oh, oh," she stutters, "yes, in a moment yes, because of my shoes, you see." And she struggles, off-balance, between the arm of Lady Merle and Flora's ministering hands slipping the shoes onto her feet, giving each ankle a little rub to reassure her. Extending one arm to the blind woman, yet oddly led by her, Eloise walks into the tower and up a winding staircase of stone.

Down in the kitchens below the tower, a broth of herbs and bones is simmering in a cauldron hanging on a hook over the fire.

Dandelions in a fallow field have closed their yellow faces for the night.

In May, the night is eight hours long, the day sixteen.
In June, the night is six hours long, the day eighteen.

JOHN WORKS IN THE CRYPT OF A CHURCH ON AN island in the middle of the river Loire. In the upcurving space between two columns, lit by small oil lamps, he is painting the image of a king, in profile. The king has stumbled, he is pitching forward, soon his crown will tumble and he will fall. A symbol of the vanities of this world. The oil lamp flickers. Kings stumble and fall. As do we all, says John to himself, repeating the words until they become a litany in his head. As do we all.

Outside the church, along the riverbank, horses are grazing under a pale sun. Every once in a while they shake their necks and step forward swishing their tails and then they lower their heads again to feed on the fresh grass. Below them the languid waters flow and flow, meandering wide.

As he works, John recalls the wonder of the days of his long pilgrimage, when he had suddenly learned to see. Wandering into a small chapel in Jaffa, he had found himself watching a man at work. An old Greek who was moving back and forth on a low scaffolding built around a pillar, applying his colours. The man had almost seemed to be dancing. And then John had seen the face of the angel coming up out of the wall, so fast that it seemed to be emerging, glistening, all by itself from the wet plaster, so fast that the man's brush seemed only to be revealing what was already there, just behind the white, a winged angel rising, head high, arms wide. And in that same instant John had known that he wanted nothing more than to do this thing, this image making, this painting, and that perhaps he had been born to do it.

John remembers telling Eloise how he learned his art, first with the Greek, for a whole year, in Jaffa, then following him for a job in a monastery in Cyprus, at Cap Gata. The place had been overrun with cats. The monks kept them to kill off the asps. He had had to work with the cats sliding past his legs. One time, purring and pushing, they had almost made him fall from a scaffolding. Eloise loved to ask him to show her how he almost fell because of the cats. He would stand with his feet close together and, pretending to be holding his brush in one hand, he would waver wildly as if he were losing his balance, and then he would make a frightened face and meow and yowl, which always sent her into peals of laughter. One day in a market, shortly before returning to France, he had come upon the fat little cloth birds stuffed with perfumed powder and bought them at once for his niece.

Little Eloise. Married. At Eastertime he had watched her walk past him in the church, her hair loose and crowned with white flowers. Once again he sees his brother pulling at her arm and pushing her hand into Robert's hand. He remembers Bernard's raspy singing voice, his back swaying slightly to the rhythm of the prayers. He sees her face as she turns for an instant toward Robert. Quick little Eloise, appraising him.

Now she sleeps in the mountains at Rochefort. Now she lives up in that blue-green pine land, up behind those dark stones. John paints the king's feet as they trip, his hands flying up in front of him. He paints the king's frightened eye.

AIMERY IS OUT OF BREATH FROM THE FALL, BUT HE must get up and try again. His horse is trembling, flaked with sweat, waiting for his signal. Aimery lifts his lance and slaps in the spurs. The beast leaps forward, and the boy does his best to keep a firm grip on the lance, aiming for the centre of the wooden mannequin. Faster, faster, keep the fist clenched, the arm firm, and aim for the round black mark, closer, closer, closer, and then a dull thud, the sound of a blow not quite on target. His lance is pushed violently to the side and the heavy figure comes swinging around and knocks him to the ground from behind. There is dust in his mouth, his shoulder aches. He picks himself up, seeking the eye of his uncle. Sure enough, Baudoin is right there, watching him from the stables, standing next to a pillar, hands on hips, a faint smile on his lips. "Again," he orders.

Aimery knows the old lord will keep him at it until he hears the resounding thunk of a bull's eye, the sound of a lance hitting dead centre, the perfectly aimed blow that will knock the wooden figure over. He has already managed to do it several times, but not every time like some of the other apprentices. He can tell that Baudoin wishes him to become as skilled as the others, that he encourages him by his presence. The tournament season is nearing, and their house is a great house. He must train and train to be worthy of the great house and the great baron who has taken him in as an apprentice.

The boy is glad of the smile on his uncle's lips, a rare sight these many months. When Aimery first came to him, greying Baudoin was still grieving the loss of his sons, both fallen in a great battle against the Muslim forces at Hittin, north of Jerusalem. Once, soon after Aimery had come, he had stumbled upon the baron in the stables. The man had fallen to his knees between two horses and he wept there, hanging on to their manes, grasping the long, rough hairs, his whole body shuddering, the tears running down into his beard and mouth. Aimery had rushed forward to try to lift him to his feet, but Baudoin had turned his head aside and ordered the boy away.

STRANGELY, IT HAD BEEN GRUFF ROBERT WHO HAD PUT a smile back onto the lord's sad face. And they all had wondered at this and also that he had given little Eloise to him in marriage. Eloise, his favourite daughter, who would have been received with joy by any of the greater barons from many valleys for miles around.

But when Robert came down from his mountain for the wedding, Baudoin had changed, suddenly finding his old voice again among his men at table. And putting an arm around Robert's neck, he had spoken to his apprentices the way he used to do, his intonations full of a singing sound they all recognized.

"You must have seen your blood run red," he had repeated to them once more in the old way, "and felt your teeth crack under a blow and been thrown to the ground again and again and felt the weight of your adversary on top of you. Twenty times you must have been thrown to the ground and twenty times gotten to your feet again! Only then will you be ready."

And they all had nodded and smiled and murmured, Yes, yes, this is so, and in their voices they let him feel their love for him and they had basked in the faithful affection that united him to Robert, who had once saved his life.

Sometimes, in the nights, the talk would go on from mattress to mattress about the baron Robert. How he was a bastard, descended from a foundling, a beautiful young girl who had caught the eye of the old mountain lord at Rochefort years before. Robert the bastard, doggedly training day after day until he had shone in Baudoin's house as the strongest of all the apprentices. A man of few words, a silent bear, a bear who had now made the lord

Baudoin laugh again and lift his cup and drink deep and recall loudly in singing tones how Robert, when they had sided with the Bishop at Mende and fought against the King of Aragon, how Robert, with a quick movement forward, had placed his shoulder between his lord and a plunging blade. There indeed was a bond.

Hand over hand, a kitchen boy is pulling up a bucket of water from the well. Water so cold, tasting of earth and rock.

A woman turns a spindle in her left hand while she pulls at the wool, twisting it between the fingers of her right hand, making a thread.

A man slips a small leather hood over the head of his falcon and places the bird on its perch for the night.

In the darkness inside a small wooden casket lies a necklace strung with nutmeg, dried roses, and violets.

THOMAS HOLDS THE SHEET OF VELLUM IN PLACE AND dips his quill into the horn of ink. He scrapes it gently, then lowers it onto the page. Grip the quill carefully now, press down, but not too hard to make the shape. From right to left, keep steady, keep the shape round, then back to the right and down again, steady, steady, another curve and there is the *S*. He puts his tongue just behind his teeth and makes the soft hissing sound of the S, like a little wind. He has practised enough on the flat boards of wax. This is a real job, this must be perfect. He is writing for the first time on vellum. The pages will make a herbarium for Bernard, who will press the dried herbs into the spaces above his words.

Still, this learning to read and write, this forming of the words, this tedious scratching, is very different from the times when he first opened his mouth and made the singing words come out from memory. Nor is it like the day, a few weeks after the lady Eloise had gone away with her new husband, when he had made himself a new and better flute and lifted it to his lips and known for sure that there was music in him and that he could make it come out with his breath and with his fingers.

He had rarely needed to listen more than once when a singer came to the castle. The words and the music stayed in his head. I have another, I have another, he would say to himself walking in the dark, going up to fire the oven in the courtyard behind the high walls. Got it, got it, he would exult, and having the song made him think of the silvery flip-flopping of a good catch when he and his father hauled up the nets. But now with these letters he knows he will be able to make many song words stay in place. They will be his always. For should he forget a line, he will have only to think of the way the words look on the page and they will come winging back to him like a falcon responding to the lure. And then, sometime soon, he will go out into the world, he will seek his way and go and go, no longer tied down to one place, to these fields under the castle and to this river. He will sing his way from place to place. Perhaps one day he will even feel the sea spray on his face and put out his tongue to taste the salty wet and know what it is to travel over the moving water.

And then perhaps he will see that mountainside in faraway Sicily that Father Bernard has told him about. A place where a belching, burning volcano sends hot stones tumbling down its flanks, rolling, rolling right down into the sea. Perhaps someday he will go there and gather up some of those light, porous stones washed up by the waves, just like the ones that Father Bernard keeps locked up in a little box. He, Thomas, will gather them up and use them to polish his own parchment pages, to make the surface of the sheep-skins smooth so that the pen moves easily. Perhaps he will even find a song of his own.

THOMAS HAD BEEN SITTING IN THE SUN ON THE riverbank mending a net and singing when the priest walked up behind him and startled him by stamping one foot and almost shouting, "Hey, boy! You there!"

Thomas had whirled around in a fright, his eyes flashing. But seeing it was only grumpy old Bernard, he relaxed at once.

"Can you sing that again?" the priest had asked in his gravelly voice.

Thomas had smiled. "I can."

"Then do so."

And so the boy had begun the song once more, and carried it as far as he knew.

Bernard had just stood there, head bowed, his arms folded across his skinny chest, listening quietly.

When Thomas was done, Bernard had said, "Do you have any idea what you are singing there, little fisherman?"

And Thomas had risen awkwardly to his feet, and standing before Bernard with the morning sun on his shock of unruly hair and stooped shoulders he had answered, "It is from a song-finder, it is from the tro-bar Perdigon."

And Bernard had smiled broadly, which looked very strange on his ugly features, and replied, "Yes, Perdigon, who came here last year. He, too, is the son of a fisherman ..."

Then there had come a silence, but Bernard had just gone on looking at Thomas, who waited, standing before him respectfully, not knowing what to say, only from time to time looking out over the moving waters and fingering the net, which had remained in his hands.

"So," said Bernard after he had studied the boy for a while. "So that is what you do when the singers come, when you creep into the big hall and sit in the ashes. You sit there and feast with your ears."

Thomas turned back toward Bernard, taking in the large, bulbous nose, the scarred skin, but also the soft brown eyes, and he suddenly saw something gleaming there, both mocking and kind, although the man had not smiled again.

"Yes," answered Thomas. And then he grinned. "A very big feast for my ears."

And so Thomas had begun tracing letters on a wax tablet under Bernard's supervision with a pointed reed. *A B C D E* ... And now he was ready for the vellum and for the quill and for the ink. *Salvia*. There. He had written his first word. *Salvia, sage.* The salvation herb. The herb that is good for everything.

SOMETIMES THOMAS THINKS THAT IT IS THE RIVER that brought him the music. As a boy he loved to listen to the different sounds it made, now rushing over rocks, now streaming through the reeds along a bank, and once, when it froze entirely, splitting and cracking like thunder with the coming of spring.

And last night he dreamed he was drifting down the river in a boat, drifting away from the familiar home place, singing a song. The boat seemed to be moving steadily of its own volition and suddenly an angel appeared before him, playing a slender flute. This angel had wide-set dark eyes and long white fingers, and in his dream Thomas sang on and on, effortlessly, as the angel played for him from the bow. Awakening, his heart racing, he wondered if the angel had come to watch over him. Yes, he said to himself. Yes. It must be so. And then he knew for sure that the time was drawing near when he would no longer be able to wait for more knowledge, when he would have to take to the road.

BERNARD'S FINGER POINTS FROM WORD TO WORD ON the page of vellum and Thomas speaks each word as Bernard points. Then, on a different sheet, Bernard points at the notes of music and Thomas sings them with not a mistake. Bernard is proud of him, Bernard is slowly closing in on him. If Thomas lets him, Bernard will try to make him a priest. Thomas does not want to disappoint Bernard, who is kind. Yes, the time will soon come when he will have to leave.

Diving down through the icy air without a sound, the nightbird plunges for a scurrying mouse. The precise claws whip the little creature up and the owl lifts off with its prey, rising and rising, floating away over the mountain forest.

In December, the night is eighteen hours long, the day six.

WINTER HOLDS THE LAND WHERE ROBERT LIVES. From fortress to fortress above the river, from valley to valley, the people stay close to their fires. There are few travellers on the roads and no boats on the river. From the high plain above Rochefort, a vast wilderness cleft with boulders, the wind whistles down through the forests and across the valleys. In those forests the beech trees are grey and bare, their naked branches rattling under the blast as the dark pines bend and sigh.

LYING ON HER BACK IN THE RUMPLED BED, ELOISE tries to remember the singing words in order to distract herself from the pains. She had first heard them sung when she was still allowed to crawl around under the big table and giggle and knock. The tale was about a young woman who had been locked up in her room, made a prisoner there by her jealous husband. The woman was closely watched by a mean old crone. And then, and then … Eloise moves her head, looking for a cool place on the pillow. The music and the words come back to her.

Every afternoon, went the song, as soon as the lady was alone, the shadow of a hawk would appear on her window ledge. When she swung the glass panes open, the hawk fluttered down into the room. But then the bird became a man, the woman's lover, and the two would come together, weeping for joy. Eloise can hear the trobar's singing voice, she can see the rapt home faces leaning forward in the candlelight. Suddenly she remembers raking at the weeds in a patch of herbs with her mother in their garden. She sees the garden clearly, the neatly boxed squares of sage, rosemary, and thyme. She feels the soft leaves of the grey-green sage under her fingers, smells their sharp, sweet smell. Salvia. The herb that saves. The herb that is good for everything.

The cry of an owl sounds from the darkness somewhere outside the fortress and Eloise feels the big wave of pain coming on again fast, then overwhelming, as her belly tightens. Down in the courtyard the midwife who was called from the village murmurs to Robert, "Your lady, how she moans." But Robert only growls at her, "Do your work, auntie, and spare me your chatter."

All day Eloise has listened for the thudding and clanking of horses and for the clatter of wagons coming up the steep road. Her mother had promised. She had said, I will be with you for the child. The owl wails again, closer this time to the tower wall.

ROBERT HAD HOPED THE CHILD WOULD COME EASILY. Now he leans back and rests his head against the rounded wall of the tower stairway and listens to the girl's muffled cries, and his heart feels like a stone. He keeps on standing there in the dark, leaning against the cold wall. He is lonely, his men all asleep in the long room above the stables, all asleep between their blankets and their mattresses. When she cries out again, he closes his eyes.

After the child is born, he decides, he will bring in a singer. Yes, he will watch for one of those wandering trobars as soon as the days begin to warm, and he will have him come to the fortress. Robert is happy with this idea, and his sturdy body relaxes slightly. He will have a singer and perhaps a juggler as well, and they will stay for a time, perhaps even a few weeks. The tro-bar with his harp in his hands will go down on one knee and sing as many tales as Lady Eloise wishes to hear, in the manner of the great courts. And the juggler will play his flute and wink and toss his painted wooden sticks and balls around and around in the air. And he will also walk on his hands to make everyone laugh. Yes, yes. And then perhaps, during those days, he will see the light come back into her eyes. Robert pictures the juggler turning cartwheels all around the room and strains for the memory of her laughter. Strains for the light he had seen in her as a child when he began to serve at her father's castle. When he had sworn to himself that this quick, slender girl would be his one day.

ELOISE FEELS TINY RIVERS OF SWEAT RUNNING DOWN through her thick and tangled hair. The village woman is back in the room; Eloise listens to her plodding feet coming closer. She smells of garlic. She is setting a basin of water on the tiles. Eloise hears the water sloshing back and forth, some of it splashing onto the floor. Now the woman's hands are moving roughly but expertly over her belly, pushing, then probing her lower down. "Not long, now, little lady," the woman whispers, and Eloise feels a cool, damp cloth come down on her forehead. "Not long, not long."

Is it a dream? she thinks wildly. Is it a dream that I am here? That I travelled up the mountain passes in a wagon covered with ribbons? That I kneel to pray with Robert on a wide stone under a rough-hewn cross? That he puts his hands on my body?

Down in the village below the fortress, in the house of a ploughman, river fish are drying in the heat of the fire, strung from their tails along the inner wall of the chimney, close to the flames. The ploughman hums a little tune to himself as he lays fresh strips of fish over the hot bricks, where he also warms his bare feet.

HER MOTHER HAS NOT COME. COULD THE CONVOY have been attacked by bandits? No, no. Her mother would travel with enough men to defend her. Why had she left her alone to bear the pains with only this garlic eater to tend to her? And Flora and the other household women, incapable, whispering and gasping behind the curtains, no good to her at all, at all. And dark Merle walking her rounds from dawn to dusk, humming her strange tunes and feeling her way up and down the winding stairs, through the kitchen, giving orders to the cook as she passes. She seems always to be walking, from the courtyard to the kitchens, from the kitchens into the stairway, up and up, from room to room, arms forever extended, as if there were eyes in her fingers, feeling her way from chair to trunk, from wall to bed. Day in and day out, day in and day out.

Her mother has not come.

ROBERT PUSHES HIMSELF AWAY FROM THE WALL. HE walks out into the courtyard. He paces between the stables and the chapel. A horseman he is, a man of arms, and he knows he is blunt and gruff. But Robert also knows that he worked long and bravely to get her. To get the highborn girl and achieve his present place in the world.

He had blocked the blow with his shoulder, taking the axe to the bone, then striking the assailant dead with one swing of his broadsword, his good arm still strong, his sharp eye knowing just where to find the opening, a whiplash slash crosswise just under the helmet. On that banner-flying day, glorious day, riot of joy in his heart, how many helmets had he battered in, sending the chain mail flying up, tainted with blood. An able and faithful fighter he is indeed. And for this he had been rewarded at last, for this he had been called to place his hands between Baudoin's hands, to swear his loyalty and receive the promise of protection in return, sealing their pledge with a kiss, mouth to mouth. For this he had been given the land, felt Baudoin press the cool clod of earth down into his palm, known that the fortress was his and the duty to keep it in this high wild country where he had been born. A good piece of the uplands. His. From the rocky heights at Falaise all the way north to the tower with its village above the river Allier. From Saint John's forest westward across the valley to the monastery at Le Vallon and all the way to the convent at Saugues that had once sheltered his mother. But above all, pride of his heart, the high fortress, the stone tower of Rochefort, with the village and fields below it, Rochefort, guarding the pass, guarding the river. And with the fortress had come at last the light-handed girl of fifteen summers, Eloise, his heart's desire, his dream of lineage and of sons. Eloise, a child running across her father's courtyard, laughing. Eloise running along the riverbank trying to catch up with her brothers. Eloise lying beside him in the wide bed with her hair undone. And the smell of rosewater on her arms, behind her small ears, in the place between her breasts.

At first he thought she might come to love his high country, and he would often ask her to accompany the hunt. But his heart sank at the sight of her pale, sad face, the quick little body become listless, drooping forward in the saddle as they rode through the forests or over the fields. He began to watch her then, like some awkward beast of prey, waiting for the slightest sign of happiness, observing her through half-closed eyes when she went to gaze out the narrow window of their bedchamber, thinking him asleep.

Early in the mornings she would sit on a high wooden stool, clasping an old cape around her shoulders, and stare out at the mountainside and at the path winding up between the trees. A path, he knew, where the peasants always walked, making loud noises with their clogs, stamping at every other step in order to frighten the wandering wolves. He had done the same as a boy. He had done the same in winter and in summer before he had had to go and get up on the stone, before his mother made him stay there for hours, just outside the fortress gate.

"Stand tall," she would hiss, pushing him up. And every time the horsemen rode out she would push him up.

"They are coming now. Hold your head high. Let them see your face."

And when the men went thundering by, she would shout the words, always the same. "This is Robert, of noble blood! Take him with you! Make him one of yours! Make him a horseman! Make him a knight!"

And one day he had indeed been taken away. His mother's stubbornness had been rewarded and he had no longer lived with her in the blacksmith's house at the base of the fortress. One day, just before his fourteenth birthday, a swarthy-faced man had stopped at last and the other riders had reined in their horses as well. The man had stared long and hard at Robert. And suddenly, as if on impulse, he had extended one arm and opened his hand. And Robert had stepped forward and grasped that arm and been pulled up onto the horse. In this way he had been taken down out of the mountains to Baudoin's big castle at La Motte. At first he had been a stable hand. But soon his skill with the beasts, his stature and brawn had proved too great a temptation for the dark-skinned sergeant, who one day handed him a broadsword and began to teach him how to use it.

Lift and parry and thrust. Lift and parry and thrust. His step was heavy but his eye was keen.

"Like a dancing bear," he had heard the sergeant say one day to Baudoin, who was watching his young trainees.

"A talented bear," came the reply. And then, in a lower voice, "Perhaps a most valuable bear." There had been no bond between them then. Baudoin's sons were still alive, the holy war had not yet taken them. But there had been a grudging admiration.

And so Robert had risen above his birth and taken up arms, he the bastard, little Robert, a snot-nosed, stub-toed, clog-wearing brat, had become a bearer of arms, a vassal, and finally a holder of land.

On impulse he enters the dimly lit chapel. A single oil lamp is flickering below the altar. Two boys from the stables lie asleep in a corner on a thick pile of hay and huddled under a blanket. He goes to the cross, kneels down on the broad stone under it, and begins the holy words. They always come to him easily, these words that he knows by heart, these words that he does not need to grapple and stumble to find. To speak his wife's name, to speak a phrase of tenderness for her, this is hard to do. And the pen marks that the monks scratch onto their pages down in the valley mean nothing to him. But the prayer words come singing up out of him and their tempo carries him away. He keeps his voice low, not to awaken the boys. Soon he no longer feels the stone under his knees.

ELOISE HAS CLOSED HER EYES, SHE CANNOT STOP HER cries. The pains are coming faster and faster. Suddenly she knows that Merle has entered the room, silent as slow water. The blind woman approaches the bed, and seizing the midwife by the shoulders she turns her around like a puppet and pushes her all the way to the wall. Now she bends down over the girl and places one hand under her neck, the other under her back. The humming sound she often makes now sounds curiously sweet and gentle to Eloise. Merle begins to move her hands very slowly under the girl's neck and shoulders, under the small of her back. Suddenly Eloise feels a sweet relief as if a river were flowing through her body. And then a rush of warm wet against her leg.

ROBERT GETS UP FROM HIS KNEES AND WALKS OUT of the chapel. There is no sound in the courtyard except the soft scraping of his boots on the paving stones. He lifts his head, breathing deeply as he looks up at the stars. And just as he releases his breath, he hears the cry of a newborn. So it is done.

He clambers up the ladder from the stables, his hands trembling as they grip the rungs, his feet slipping, his heart racing. In the long hall he runs quickly and lightly between his sleeping men and plunges into the circular stairway, up and up, two by two, three by three. Emerging into the big round room at the top of the tower he passes his mother and, barely touching her hands in greeting, strides toward the bedchamber and throws aside the heavy woolen curtain.

The midwife, startled, turns to him. In her arms, still loosely wrapped in a white linen cloth, a mewing infant struggles and wails, raising its clenched fists. On the floor beside her a cloth floats in the basin of water red with blood. Beyond, in the bed, the girl lies still, her face turned away toward the narrow window. "A boy," says the midwife. "A fine boy." Her eyes are bright with relief as she hands him the little one. The dark lady is allowing her to take the credit for the successful birth. Robert holds the newborn awkwardly, staring down into its tiny face, feeling the warm life quivering into his hands.

He gives the bundle back to the woman. She cradles it with a soft clucking of her tongue, and this clucking sound that only peasants make cuts at his heart. But now he is beyond the trudging and the banging of the clogs. He will never again walk a mountain path in fear of the wolves. He rides a high horse, he raises a sword, his word is heeded. And now he has a son.

One step and he is beside her. "Lady," he whispers, kneeling, and then "Eloise," able to speak her name in the urgency of the instant. Her arms lie over the covers, her hands open, weary, still. She turns toward him but does not seem to see what she is looking for in his face. She tries to smile and then she closes her eyes without a word. He releases her hand, lays it back down on the cover.

"Keep the fire going strong," he growls to the midwife, and he rises to his feet and walks out of the room.

The ploughman turns the strips of fish. They are soaking up the heat and the smoke. Soon they will be ready to eat. In the shadows behind him, his wife traces a cross on the bread, then slices two portions. The ploughman rubs his feet, his knees, his hands. He spreads his fingers before the flames.

THOMAS LEANS FORWARD. BERNARD HAS OPENED THE tall book, he is going to allow him to see this wonder. Thomas begins at the top of the page, moving slowly down from one picture to the next. God is making the world. First he is making the light. Then he is dividing the light from the dark. Now he is making the great arc of the sky and now he is bringing the dry land up out of the waters. Here are the grasses and the trees as they come greening up out of the earth with their seeds and their fruits. It is all there in bright colours on the parchment page; Thomas can follow the making from image to image. God is setting the sun into the sky and now the moon and now the stars. And now all the animals, the great whales that move through the seas and the birds that fly through the air and all the other beasts of the earth. One, two, three, four, five, six, seven. Seven pictures, each picture in a round, one for each of the seven days. They shine up at him in blues and reds, in whites and greens. God is making Adam, the first man, and now he is pulling Eve, the first woman, from Adam's side. Finally, on his golden throne and surrounded by a shimmering light, God sits and rests and blesses the seventh day. Bernard is praying.

Thomas goes down the images again, stopping to feast his eyes on each one. He is grateful to Bernard, but he knows that the time is coming for his going.

Bernard is trying to keep him from leaving, but it is time, time, time for him to walk out into the world.

DEEP IN THE MOUNTAIN FOREST ACROSS THE VALLEY from Robert's fortress stands a crude hut of logs and branches. It has been built near a little spring. Behind the mossy door a man is moving, slipping a leather pouch over his shoulder. He bends over a wooden bucket beside the door, breaks the ice with his fist, and lowers a clay bowl into the water. The man drinks, drops the bowl into his pouch, grasps a stick, smooth with use, and pushes his way out the door into a clearing. The man is bearded, a cloak of animal skins hangs from his shoulders. He resembles the wild, he is a mass of walking vegetation and fur with eyes that shine like a bird's eyes. He strides away and disappears between the dark pines and the grey trunks of the beech trees.

How long since he left the monastery, how long since he laid away pen and penknife and stopped working on the charts? The carefully drawn and many-coloured charts used to calculate the seasons and the holy days. How long since he heard anyone speak his name, Brother William, Brother William. How long since he walked with the others behind the candles and the incense, moving together from the church to the chapter, from the refectory to the church, where they did their singing for the world, all day, every day, and in the deep of the night, every night.

Kyrie eleison …
In excelsis Deo …

How long since he chose the wilderness?

Sometimes he allows himself to think of the places he has left behind, a world where people are always together, moving in groups, heads bowed in prayer, heads bobbing in a dance, high heads flung back, riding to war or to the games of war. Low heads in the fields, backs bent forward with the sun beating down on them in summer, freezing winds cutting through their clothes in winter, making them run to huddle around their fires as soon as they can.

Just before the midday meal, the brother cooks would always leave the choir quickly and discreetly to go and spoon the hot food from the big cauldron into the bowls, usually portions of lentils and lard. They would set the full bowls out onto the table, a spoon beside each bowl. He remembers the thudding as the bowls were set down one after the other onto the table at each brother's place, and the taste of the wooden spoon against his teeth and tongue. And how, keeping to the rule of silence, he would make the sign for bread, joining forefingers and thumbs together to form a circle. And then extending one hand to receive his pittance.

Once the days had been jolted by an execution at the abbey. He had watched the beheading from behind a column. He should have been at his prayers, but he had watched. And later, his body trembling from pity and rage, he could not erase from his mind's eye the image of what he had seen. The condemned man was an old drunk who had beaten his son to death. Yet William was haunted by the miserable kneeling old man, the descending sword, the gush of blood, the still body on the ground like a rag doll. It was then he had first begun to think of solitude.

Singing of the psalms began at matins in the heart of the night, then at lauds to greet the light, then prime, terce, and on through the hours, terce, sext, none, vespers, until at last, after compline, as the darkness moved over them, they would give themselves up exhausted, to the silence, abandon themselves all into the hands of God. He had loved his life inside these hours. Yet, soon after witnessing the execution, something irrepressible had begun to stir in him and he had requested permission to live as a hermit. And his request had been granted.

In the spring he will clear ground and plant a few things, cabbage, onions, perhaps some turnips. He will continue to gather all he can find, all the forest can give. The wild apples, the wild berries, and the watercress around the spring. Wind and snow are his brothers now, sun and rain he calls his sisters. Even the wolves howling from the upper reaches have entered his prayers, as have the foxes, the badgers, and the soaring hawks.

"Ave Maria," he murmurs, falling to his knees, pressing his lips hard against the snowy ground.

BABEL IS HUNGRY. HE SITS BY THE FIRE, WAITING, watching for his chance. Every once in a while, if someone looks over at him, he smiles and raises his shoulder bag, shaking it a little so the jingling and rattling of the bells and the wooden balls inside can be heard. He wants to shout, "Juggler, juggler!" but this could get him into trouble. Someone must ask. So he sits and waits and smiles, his stomach growling so loudly he wonders that no one can hear it. After a time, he turns away and stares at the fire.

Suddenly he feels a tap on his shoulder. A young man with a shock of curly hair is looking down at him.

"Give us a laugh, boy, and I'll feed your belly."

The words are common, but the young man's eyes show something else.

Babel reaches into his bag for the painted wooden balls. He slips the bells around his ankles.

He rises to his feet in the firelight and begins to juggle. First he throws up a single ball, then two, then three, then four. Babel keeps them spinning around and around as he begins to move from side to side, the little bells jingling as he hops and dances. Around and around they go in front of the crackling flames. Then suddenly he lets them fall, catching them two by two neatly behind his back, and, pitching forward, rolls them into his bag. Now he vaults up onto his hands. Legs in the air, he makes his way around the smoke-filled room, chanting a nonsense verse he picked up on his travels:

> *I go hunting rabbit,*
> *while riding on an ox!*
> *I swim against the current!*
> *I sing to a fox!*
> *And I capture the wind,*
> *the wind, the wind.*
> *Ha ha ha!*
> *I capture the wind!*

Here and there, people clap and laugh. Someone slaps at his backside for a joke but he does not lose his balance. When he jumps to his feet again, the young man calls to him from across the room, shouting, "Over here!" He has made a place for him at his table. A thick slice of bread lies there next to a steaming bowl. As Babel swings one leg over the bench, he sees there is also a jug of wine. "Please, help yourself," the young man is saying. "My name is Thomas."

Babel spoons up the lentils and takes a bite out of the bread. He chews and swallows quickly, having had nothing to eat for two days.

"They call me Babel," he explains between bites. "Because I speak so many different languages. From my *viajos*. My travels. And because I am always mixing them up." The boy grins and lifts the jug of wine. "I will be speaking in langue d'oc and then suddenly find myself in Spanish or in Arabic! But I cannot help it. I grew up with a troupe of musicians from many places and their voices all live in my head! *In'ch Allah!*"

"Eat, eat," says Thomas, leaning forward. "When you are finished, I want you to tell me what you can do."

ROBERT LIES ON A MATTRESS AMONG HIS MEN. THEIR shields hang on the wall side by side, the fire hums and crackles. He reminds himself that he has a coat of arms for all to see, a soaring falcon on a field of blue. There are no shadows in his hall when darkness reigns outside. No man goes hungry who is in his care. Yet he is struck down, struck dumb as a mute, having heard her as he climbed the stairs, stopped in his footsteps knowing she was sobbing up there, bent double in the middle of the bed, pushing her face down into the fur of the bedcover to muffle the sound of her crying. It was a childish sound, she still cried like a child, and he knew that the fur would be wet where her tears were sliding down and he knew that she wept because of him, tongue-tied and clumsy, stupid in her eyes, stupid and gruff. That she wept because this was to be her lot, her place on fortune's wheel. Surely she was feeling herself spinning down and down. It was only much later, many days after the birth of the boy, that he had thought of the words he wished he had spoken to her. My love for you is without end, like the sky. Now he would never say them.

Snow has begun to fall. It gathers in shifting drifts on the flat stones at the top of the tower and on the window ledges farther down. It blows into the faces of the saints over the doorway of the chapel and onto the thatched roofs huddled close to the rocks at the base of the tower walls. It gathers on the beehives standing in a row behind the blacksmith's house. It gathers on the haystacks in the little field beyond. A cat runs from under a beehive toward the house. Its tracks are quickly filled.

DESPERATELY ROBERT CALLS UP THE SIGHT OF HIS banners, his red falcon, his blue sky. And the glow of the candles over his table, the glimmering of the torches on his walls, the hands of a servant pouring water over his fingers before each meal, the taste of wine on his tongue. By the living Christ is he not a baron now, damn her tears! Should she not be grateful to him and greet him with shining eyes and ride with the hunt, lithe, erect, and laugh and break into song with the others? Hadn't she laughed and trembled in his arms the day he told her how he once killed a wild bear single-handed? Hadn't she cried out in a high voice, a voice filled with wonder, when he told her how he had gone at the beast with a lance and how the blood had run down over his hands? And didn't she sometimes slide her little fingers along the scars on his shoulder and on his arm, the battle scars and those from the beast's long claws? Sliding and sighing, So brave, my dear lord, so brave.

Greater feats will come to him, he swears. He pictures himself a crusader before the holy city, before the lost Jerusalem, flying up the walls on the lances of his men. This would be greatness to awe her at last. He opens his eyes. From one end of the long room to the other, his men, his companions, sleep rolled into their blankets. Some snore, one must be dreaming because he groans and sighs. Tonight Robert has chosen to remain here, to leave the lady up there at the top of the tower with her mother and her mother's ladies and the wailing newborn. He will not go up there to lie beside her tonight. Tonight he will keep the company of his men.

The ploughman and his wife sleep close, body to body against the cold. The cat is curled up by the fireplace near the glowing embers. From time to time one of its ears twitches.

In January, the night is sixteen hours long, the day eight.
In February, the night is fourteen hours long, the day ten.

"GRAN, GRAN, TELL ONE ABOUT THE FOX," PIPES A child's voice, a boy. The blacksmith's family is huddled around a crackling fire, the only light in the cottage room. The winter wheat has been planted. The baron Robert is home. All is well. Their bodies are weary, but they have had enough to eat, warm porridge and some bread.

"Go on, Gran," says the other boy. "Tell the one where the fox makes the wolf go fishing with his tail."

The old woman adjusts herself on the bench. "You want that one, do you?"

"Yes, that one!" cries the little girl. "The one you used to tell to Merle when she was a girl, before she went up to the fortress to be the lady. The one that made her laugh."

"Go on, Ma," says the smith, pressed up close

against his wife for extra warmth, their arms around each other's waists.

The old woman chuckles. "Brother Fox played a good trick there. It was a winter day, much like today, and the pond had frozen over. And that's what gave the fox his idea of how to get back at the wolf. So as soon as he saw the wolf ambling by he called out to him, 'Brother Wolf, dear friend, I can tell you how to catch a great many fish.' And Wolf, who wasn't any too clever, answered, 'Oh? Tell me at once!'

"So Fox takes Wolf out into the middle of the pond and he says, 'Now look, do you see this hole in the ice? And this bucket? I am going to tie the bucket to your tail and you have only to put your tail down into the hole and the fish will all come into the pail and you will just pull them up by the dozen!'"

The children begin to giggle, the parents are smiling.

"Old Wolf sits down on the ice and puts his tail with the bucket down into the hole. Fox cries, 'Good luck, my brother!' and darts off into the bushes at the edge of the pond to watch and wait. Sure enough, the fish come tickling, tickling around that tail, and soon the wolf thinks—"

"That the pail is full of fish!" cries the little girl.

"Exactly so!" says the grandmother. "Now after a

time Wolf's rear end is frightfully cold from sitting on that ice. And he says to himself, 'There must be enough fish in this bucket. I am going to pull it up.' But when he tries to get up, the pond has frozen solid around his tail, and he is stuck there, most terribly stuck!"

"Most terribly stuck!" shout the children.

"And Fox is laughing to split his sides!" concludes the old woman.

The family rises, and clumping in their clogs, they make for their blankets and their straw mats. Gran has shared hers with her granddaughter since the old man died, and the parents lie down on the bigger one with the boys. Soon they are all asleep. No one mentioned the lady Merle again. They all knew how it had been with Merle, how the old baron had brought her to the house when Gran was a young woman, just barely married, and Merle already a child of eleven. How Gran had taken care of her and how Merle had lived with them for all those years after Robert was taken away by the horsemen. Just before drifting off, the old woman hears laughter out of the past, high and sweet, she sees the young girl running out the door into the sunlight, her long black hair swinging from side to side.

Snow can still be seen on the ground here and there, but a wagon labouring up the road to the fortress leaves mud at the bottom of the furrows made by its wheels. A squirrel darts into the wagon tracks. It finds a half-frozen acorn, cracks the shell, and nibbles at the nutmeat.

The man driving the wagon shouts and whistles at the oxen and slaps their backs with a long, dry switch. Three helmets with chain-mail skirts roll around in the rear beside sacks of dried beans and a ploughshare.

In the garden behind the walls of the fortress five fruit trees are growing, three apple and two pear. The sunlight has caused blossoming to begin even though there is still a smell of winter in the air.

MERLE COMES UP THE SPIRAL STAIRWAY, HER HANDS pressed against the wall to feel her way. She wants to touch his little feet again. The ladies' voices sound like small bells tinkling. One more step up, one more and one more. She can feel the warmth in the room, she knows that the spring sunlight is bringing part of this heat. She cannot see the young girl reclining near the fire with the child asleep at her breast and her hair all undone, but the voices tell her much.

Standing behind Eloise, one of the ladies combs and braids the girl's wild curls. The mother sits close beside her daughter, Merle is certain of this. Close beside her, the two of them leaning against each other. This woman will not leave soon. Merle listens to her voice as she croons and hums, sweet, sweet. Perhaps to the girl, perhaps to the child, perhaps to them both.

Merle walks forward so that all must notice her presence. Chattering ceases, needles pulling fine thread remain suspended, pearled heads click as they turn, silken sleeves rustle.

"Ah, my lady Merle," murmurs the mother, rising and walking toward the older woman. "Come, give me your hand and sit beside us."

Now Merle can smell the child's milky smell and for a few instants she holds him, feels his wet mouth against her cheek. Of course they know about her, all these gentlewomen. She cradles the baby. The talk has begun again. Although no one speaks to her directly, except from time to time the mother of the girl, she is given due respect. Still, all that goes unspoken weighs on her heart. Robert the bastard. Protected by the great Baudoin. And only because of this is she tolerated. Could they know everything? How she got her son, down on the beds of soft sand, down where the river flows between walls of rock? And how she made him what he is, pushing him up on the stone, shouting at the barons as they passed?

In the mountain fields the ploughing has begun. The ploughman wields a long stick with his left hand to keep the oxen in line. His right hand grips the handle of the plough. Urging the animals forward, now with a shrill whistle, now in deep tones, he forces the

ploughshare down as the beasts strain in their traces and the turn-
ing up and up of the earth begins, up and out, up and out, the mold-
boards pushing the moving earth to the right and to the left from one
end of the field to the other.

The sower walks barefoot behind the ploughman along the ridges
of earth, throwing out the seed. He reaches into the pouch hanging
from his waist and grasps the small, dry kernels of wheat by exact
handfuls, flinging them out in arcing showers to the rhythm of his
walking. His bare feet leave prints in the fresh soil.

MERLE HOLDS THE BABY, HIS LITTLE HAND IS GRIPPING
one of her fingers, but then she hears the lady's smooth
voice, a voice accustomed to giving orders in a vast
house, "Come now, come now, let me have him," and
the little one is lifted away and her arms are empty
once more. Still she sits beside them, listening to their
talk, her own story turning and twisting inside her like
some animal trying to escape. This beast, she must
keep it quiet. Keep it quiet and smile and listen from
her darkness while they hum and chatter and sew.
From time to time, all their voices come together in a
little song while she sits with bowed head pulling at her
fingers and taking it all into herself, their voices, their
perfume, and the smells of spring from the narrow
window.

He had always come in the night when she lived in

the cottage at the base of the fortress. He would scratch at the wall with a stone. Sometimes he would come right in, stumbling past her foster parents' bed, whispering and groping for her in the dark. No one dared resist. He was the baron. No one ever spoke a word to him.

After a time she began to slip outside and wait for him. Down to the river they would ride together on one horse. They would stay there for hours and hours. Down past the cliffs where the water rushes and roars between walls of rock, down to the beds of soft sand, the place where the river becomes a silent flow. She knows they are still there, those beds. That is where he went with her, the man who kept the fortress in those days, tall Anselme, Robert's father, the mountain lord.

When she told him about the coming child he had laughed and kissed her full on the lips and shouted at the swift waters, "One for the stables, my forest girl, one for the fields, one for the kitchens, as many as you want!" But then he had died at war in a faraway place, and the lord Baudoin had sent a new man from the valley to keep the fortress. She had hoped for something, she knew not what exactly, but they had pushed her out of the hall with loud shouting when she had dared to come up to the fortress with the newborn child.

"Out of here with your bastard!" they had shouted.

"She thinks she is a lady!" cried another. Someone had grabbed at her, trying to touch her breasts. "We'll all be down to see you, great lady," he had cried out. They had never molested her, but their laughter had rung in her ears for weeks on end.

After a time, the idea of the mounting stone had come to her. For as the boy grew older, he became the very image of his father. Shorter, broader through the shoulders, but the very image nevertheless. And so, every time the horsemen would ride out of the fortress, she would be there, pushing her child up on the ancient stone next to the gate, the first ever used in that place, so the story went, to help a man get onto a horse. "Stand tall, Robert!" she would whisper. "Remember, you are of noble blood. Stand tall and look them in the eye!"

Merle stirs in her chair and rises to her feet. There is scarcely a ripple in the women's conversation as she nods and feels her way out of the room. She must get away, she must go and lie down. Her head has begun to ache. But soon the forest people will come to dance and whisper around her, taking away the pain and comforting her with their presence as they often do when she is sad. Their fleeting melodies lift her spirits and from her darkness she can see them whirling and dancing, the people who move between the leaves. Perhaps they really are her people after all, not these churchfolk. Perhaps, she dares to think, the dreams that sometimes take hold of her are true and she really came from them so long ago when Anselme found her lying in the crook of a willow tree, a newborn child. Perhaps they have been trying to get her back, little by little, by bringing on this darkness.

In the wheatfields where the young shoots have emerged, a cadenced thumping interrupts the labour. The ploughmen turn their heads anxiously toward the sound of horsemen. The riders emerge from behind a rocky rise at the far end of the field. Sunlight flashes from their helmets as they cross and then plunge into a little wood. When they can no longer be heard, the peasants resume their work, relieved that they are gone.

Now a boy is running along the path in the forest where the horsemen thundered through. Branches have been ripped from the greening oaks and birches. The boy darts along, picking them up. These will be good, these will be perfect. He will tie them to his head and shoulders tomorrow when he dresses as the forest spirit. Tomorrow is the first day of May. He will be in the centre of the round of dancers and they will turn and turn, their feet pounding the ground, and they will sing and cheer him on as he whirls, a blur of hands and leaves.

In May, the night is eight hours long, the day sixteen.
In June, the night is six hours long, the day eighteen.

ROBERT LIES AMONG HIS MEN, HIS BACK RESTING against a tree, their camp spread out along the river. The sun is going down and he smells woodsmoke and roasting meat from the cooking fires, but he is not hungry. His thigh burns under the poultice; he is tired. He saw death up close today, felt it in his parched mouth and behind his eyes. But he is alive. His experience tells him that this wound will heal. He will live to see Eloise again, and his son.

The castle had fallen to them, the rebellious baron had been slain, his wife and children taken hostage. On Baudoin's orders, Robert had thrown a torch up onto one of the village roofs below the walls when the old peasant had rushed at him with an axe. One turn in the saddle, one thrust of his broadsword, and the fellow lay dead, but then Robert had looked down and seen his own thigh bleeding in spurts from the well-aimed blow. All around him the fires were hissing and crackling high. Had his time come? Suddenly Robert had felt a strange peace wash over him and he had thrown his head back to look up and see if the skies were opening, to see if he could catch sight just for an instant of what lay beyond. But the pain had forced him to return to himself. The people from the flaming village had begun running to the church for safety, shouting to each other. And his boy was crying,

"Baron, baron, a bad wound! Very bad!" and running, leading his horse quickly away from the fray.

Now the old herb woman, moving from tent to tent, hobbles toward Robert with her basket of remedies.

"Better?" she asks. "Shall I renew the bandage?"

Robert is listening to the running waters of the river. Somewhere in the camp a man has begun to sing in a high voice, sharp and clear, of banners yellow, indigo, and blue.

"No, leave me be," he says. "In the morning, perhaps."

How had he not seen the coming blow? An aching and a heaviness is pulling at his heart. He hopes the old fellow died at once. Certainly, he thinks to himself, certainly he made a clean kill. But if he had been more alert, this would not have happened at all. Robert shuts out the sounds of shouting and burning that keep rolling over him. This killing of helpless peasants grinds at his heart. He lived too long with them as a child. It dulls his love for Baudoin, who does not care how many ploughmen he kills. Still, Robert chides himself. He should have been quicker. Had he been quicker, he would never have been wounded and the old man would not be dead. The poor fellow could have reached the church or scuttled off between the trees and taken refuge in the wild. Perhaps the girl is to blame, perhaps she lives too much in his thoughts and robs him of alertness. Perhaps he should keep his distance for a time. The sound of flowing water is filling him with sleep, and he drifts off until the boy comes and helps him into his tent for the night.

In Robert's vineyards, the pruning is done. Now the plants need only sufficient rain and a good increase of sun for the grapes to swell and darken, so many on the vine. And for the wheat to ripen in the fields so that no hunger can come.

THE SPRING WIND IS BRINGING EARTH SMELLS FROM the forest and the fields. Spurring his horse forward, Robert feels his body as one with the animal as it plunges ahead in quick response to his touch, as one with the reins running tight through his palms and fingers. The wild boar is straight ahead of him now. Pushing to a full gallop, Robert releases the reins, stretches high in the saddle, no pain from the wound to his thigh, and exultantly he strains the bow and lets the arrow fly. It strikes true, and the rushing beast drops to its knees, a clean kill. Thundering up from behind him, his men shout their admiration for this perfect shot. Now the dogs are baying in Robert's ears and his companions encircle him and he himself shouts with them until their shouting turns to laughter under the trees and sky.

Riding back to the fortress, Robert allows himself to

think about her. About the child, their son, as well, but more about her, even though these thoughts will take away his laughter. He allows himself to picture her small, oval face, her white, white skin and the rosewater smell of her hands on his face and mouth and her thick, dark hair all springy with curls when released from its braids, and her body, still childish in spite of the pregnancy, her body opening under him with never, ever a sigh. And always turning away afterward, turning away toward the narrow window, then creeping over to her perch and staring out at the forest as he slips into sleep.

ELOISE LOOKS UP AT THE SKY FROM HER PERCH beside the narrow window and she hears the shouting and the whooping from her husband and his men. She can detect the fierce elation in their voices; this is what brings them joy. A breeze runs over her and she breathes it in. Behind her, beyond the heavy curtain, in the big round middle room, her mother is singing something to little John.

She is pleased to have given the child her uncle's name; somehow it gives her a feeling of peace. Suddenly Eloise begins to listen more carefully to her mother's humming. The tune sounds familiar and then she remembers. It is the oven boy's song, that skinny boy with a hawk nose, that Thomas, the fisherman's son,

who came to light the fire every morning before day-
break from the time she was a little girl. He had always
piped that little chant in the darkness in his high, clear
voice. She remembers how she used to call and chirp
and whistle at him and peer out to catch a glimpse of
his shadowy form bent over the rounded mass of the
bread oven, slipping in the twigs until the first tiny
flickerings appeared. And she hears the familiar childhood sound, the thump of the logs as he pushed them
in, followed by the hum of the flames.

"*To ask your way,*" he had quavered, "*if this you know, if this
you know, through all the world, your steps may go.*" The oven boy.
She wonders if he is still at home, working the river,
pulling up his nets.

*Now that the spring weather has begun, the fire stays low in the
ploughman's house once the evening soup has cooked. He and his
wife don't need the flames anymore to keep the damp away. Just a
few embers. The ploughman sits on a stool, his weary hands hanging loose between his knees, and he watches the glowing in the dimness
of the dusk coming in from the open door. It is neither day nor night,
it is the hour "between dog and wolf."*

WHEN HER MOTHER HAD ARRIVED AT LAST, REACHING
Rochefort a day too late for the birth, Eloise had for-
given her at once, basking in the familiar, somewhat

heavy footsteps, in her soft kisses, in her lavender smell. Lady Agnes had admired everything, the sculpted trunks, the bedcovers of satin and fur, the tapestry on the wall in the bedchamber. "A fine piece of work," she had said. "Very fine," she had repeated, with unnecessary insistence.

That same night, as Eloise had put her child to the breast for the first time, felt his little mouth pulling, felt the milk flowing, the mountain wind had begun to blow, and by morning it had been strong enough to push a man to the ground.

Now, even after the passing of time, Eloise remembers how that wind had made her sob. "You see, you see, how hard it is here." And her mother had tried to comfort her, saying, "It is only a wind. Look at your child. Hold him."

Now her mother is with her once again. They are sitting together on the bed. Eloise, half reclining, has laid her head on her mother's lap.

"Sometimes," she says in a low voice, "Lady Merle wanders up and down the stairway at night. She comes into our room and she runs her hands over his face and sometimes she comes around to my side of the bed and slides her hands over the covers. Once she touched my face too and I was so frightened I almost shouted, but I didn't want to wake Robert."

Agnes says nothing for a moment. And then she begins to stroke her daughter's hair. "This woman," says Agnes, choosing her words carefully, "there is no evil in her, only suffering. She will never harm you. And she helped you greatly in the birth. Do not forget that."

Eloise touches the fine weave in her mother's dress, running her fingers around a pattern of roses and leaves. "I long for home," she whispers.

Lady Agnes does not answer her daughter. She takes the girl's hand and strokes it quietly. Then she rises, pushes Eloise into a sitting position, and begins to undo her braids.

"Let us brush your lovely hair," she says. "Let us breathe the spring air."

Down by the river, after the last rapids, down where the trees send their silvery shadows over the water, the winds are still warm even though the sun has gone down. There has been dancing, and now, along the bank, the village people have built a fire. Some of the men and women are wading out into the water, leaving their clothing folded in little piles near the firelight. With only the green tendrils wound around their heads, they step and feel their way into the stream, their toes gripping at the rocks and the sand, until the water is flowing under their arms and up to their necks, until they begin to drift and float, free of weight and free of labour in the warm June night.

Eloise sleeps and dreams. In her dream she is standing before a bed of cedar wood inlaid in ivory and engraved in gold. A wounded man is lying in the bed. She is pouring water into a golden basin. The man's wound is near the heart. She is washing this wound and wiping away the blood with a fine linen cloth. But the man is dying, and suddenly in her dream she recognises him as the man of the bird shadow. The man in the song from her childhood. The knives placed on the outside wall have killed him, the knives placed there by her jealous husband. Her lover has been mortally wounded. Flying to join her, he has been killed. She washes and washes, but the man is dying.

Eloise wakes up in tears. She cannot hold back a sob. Robert's sleep is disturbed, he opens his eyes and sees her weeping. He seizes her roughly by the shoulders then, and, his fingers crushing through her flesh and into her bones, whispers slowly, "I go to any door for miles around and they bow and make a place for me. For me! Do you hear?"

The village people open their mouths and drink from the river flowing over their lips. A garland of leaves falls from a woman's loosened hair and floats slowly away. It floats down past the monastery where a tall monk stands looking out over the water, studying the place where he plans to build a mill. With a melancholy smile, he watches the garland pass.

THOMAS IS CROSSING A FOREST, FOLLOWING A well-worn path. He feels no fear in this mountain country where old Baudoin's rule extends like a king's. He begins to work through a song to the rhythm of his walking, the words rising to his lips, now only faintly, just for memory's sake, now with more feeling until his singing voice sounds out, rising and falling under the whispering blue pines. Thomas has the harp slung in its pack across his shoulders. The harp, his voice, and the songs, that is all his fortune now. A good strong voice, he knows, that carries well, a voice that fills the great halls right up to the rafters and into the farthest corners where the spiders sleep. A good voice and a long memory where the stories live, ready for his listeners to make them dream or laugh or weep. The figures in these tales have become his friends and he speaks to them and in his mind they answer him, calling him by name, Thomas.

As he works through his song, he catches the sensations from his tale and feels the great ship heaving through the sea. In that song story the day is warm and the lovely girl is reaching for the silver cup and lifting it to her lips. She drinks and then offers the goblet to the young man beside her and he drinks as well. Neither of them realise what they have done, they were only thirsty, but now the potion in the drink is running into their veins.

The wind goes on whispering through the trees over Thomas as he walks, while in his song another wind swells a sail and pushes the two lovers forward in the belly of the ship. The young man named Tristan must complete his mission and take the beautiful girl named Isolde to marry his uncle, the king, though all now is utterly changed for them and they can no longer bear to be apart.

Thomas stops, walks on a while in silence, listening to the sound of rushing water from the river below. And then he begins again. A boy with quick movements trots along behind him, keeping his distance. Every once in a while, the little fellow whistles between his teeth and takes a skip and a jump as if he were dancing, and his arms fly up as if he were throwing his coloured sticks and balls into the air, his feet pounding the boards of a platform set up in a village square. But Babel knows that he must keep quiet when Thomas is working. They have been travelling together for several months now and are used to each other's ways.

The boy feels lucky to have joined up with such a singer. Lucky to have been noticed by him on that hungry day at the inn. Truly a fine performer with so many tales in his head, and knowing his letters as well. And a strong voice, firm and melodious. People talk about them now. Thomas and Babel, they say. Thomas and Babel are much in demand. The boy knows he is agile, a fine juggler with a gift for mimicry, but he knows too that it is the trobar who brings success. Still, he reassures himself, we make a good team. Perhaps the partnership will last for a few more seasons, at least through the coming summer. Yes, certainly through the summer.

EMERGING FROM THE FOREST, THOMAS IS BRIEFLY blinded by the sunlight. As his eyes grow accustomed to the light he notices a group of horsemen on the road below. He has started down the path when suddenly one of them raises a shout. Thomas keeps walking down the path, but when he reaches the road, he stands and waits, observing the man of arms as he spurs his horse forward, raising dust and leaving a small group of companions behind him.

Now the man on horseback is looking down at him, holding the snorting animal in check and peering intently, dark eyes in a black-bearded face. Shifting his weight in the saddle, the man speaks in quick phrases, as if talking were something he wished to get over with as quickly as possible.

"God save you, trobar!"

Babel comes running down now, with his pack of bells and wooden balls and sticks, making a knocking, clinking sound as he approaches. The horseman studies the new arrival.

"God save both of you!" he says in a louder voice. "I am Robert of Rochefort. I keep the fortress above the river to the north there. I wish you to come for a few days. I will pay you in coin and feed you into the bargain with a place to sleep close to the fire. I wish you to come and sing for my lady—" And with that last word he stops for an instant before adding, "—for my lady and for us all."

Babel blurts, "We are expected elsewhere in a week's time, at the great court in—"

"I will give you horses," the rider interrupts impatiently. "And cloth as well as coin, if you come to us."

Thomas stares at the horseman. Robert. Married to Eloise. A bright head at the high table and Thomas in the ashes listening.

"We will come to you," he says.

TODAY THERE IS A CHANGE IN THE SOUNDS THAT reach her from below. Eloise has heard something, something unaccustomed has entered the fortress. She listens again. Between the clanking of chains and the stamping and the blowing of the horses, between the clucking of the chickens and the shouting from man to man, someone is tuning a harp. And now someone is playing a flute, high and clear. Yes, again, from below there comes a piping, a strumming. Little John stirs in the cradle at her side. Eloise pushes her feet into the shaft of summer sunlight that is illuminating the tiles where the image of a laughing fox stops and runs, stops and runs. The piping sounds again, a distinct melody, and then she hears a man's singing voice, rising and falling. Her body shivers and she inadvertently pricks her finger with the needle. She puts her finger into her mouth at once, to avoid staining her work. Someone plays, someone sings. Could it be a trobar, one of the wanderers? The taste of blood is in her mouth. She feels her heartbeat quicken, the pulse at her temples where her tightly bound braids are pulled back and wound around her head. Suddenly the tears well up in her eyes. "I can never go home," she breathes. Yet, in spite of the seasons she has already lived in the fortress with Robert, she imagines the journey again and again.

Sometimes she sees herself on a fine white mare, with a flowing silken mane, and she is riding away from the fortress and down the steep mountain road, down past the great forked tree where hunters perch in the winter for hours, waiting for wolves. Past the monastery where the monks chant their prayers for the world. Past the convent and the wheatfields and the vineyards.

Once again she sees herself going down and down, out of the wild land and back to her own valley. She can almost feel the warm home winds on her neck.

A fly is buzzing on the window ledge. Eloise watches it flit forward, the successive bursts of its tiny energy. She, the fly, her child, the windowsill, the sun, her husband, her sister Hedwige, who has come to stay for the summer—all are in God's hands, she says to herself, each one of us in his place. Yet the tears come unbidden.

The long winter is past, she repeats to herself, and listens to the sound of the streams running down through the fields all around the fortress, hundreds of streams flowing out of the mountain springs, swollen by the melting snows and running down through the grasses, rushing finally to meet the river that surges and roars between walls of rock before winding out into the valley. Eloise licks at a tear, tastes its saltiness, then straightens up and wipes her eyes.

The narrow shaft of sunlight from the window has moved. It lights the tapestry hanging on the wall. A lady in a dress of blue and red rides there on a dappled grey. Leaning slightly forward, the lady carries a hawk on her gloved wrist. The sunlight is falling directly onto the lady and her bird, leaving their followers in shadow. The colours in the tapestry, red and green, and blue and darker blue, lift her spirits. The voice sounds again and her sister pushes aside the curtain.

"Eloise, do you hear?" she says, smiling. "Can you believe it? We have a trobar down below!"

At the bottom of the valley in Robert's vineyards, three village men in wide straw hats are replacing some of the poles that hold up the vines. Their hammers knock against the oak as they pound these new stakes into the ground. Near them, another man works at the vines with his curved knife, slicing away the shoots bearing no grapes, or too few.

JOHN PAINTS THE SERPENT'S TAIL, CAREFULLY OUTlining its many coils and scales, working with his brushes in green and black. Even after a whole week, relief still floods his body. He is grateful to the monks, to the abbot. They had let him in, given him refuge. A cot to sleep on in the long dormitory, under the rafters, a place at the table, food, work.

He paints carefully, taking his time. He feels safer now from his great sin with the prayers going up all around him day and night and the bells ringing out the hours. He is sad because he cannot go to visit Eloise. She doesn't even know that he is here. But he must complete his penance. He thinks of her as a little girl, thinks of how her eyes kept opening and closing, night after night, as he told his tales from the holy land. Now she lives up on that mountain married to gruff Robert. John pushes the thought of his niece out of his mind.

He plans the figure of a little monkey, perched up in the branches of a flowering tree. The monkey will be red, he decides, and the birds yellow and blue. Still working on the snake he imagines the many opening leaves he will give to the tree and also its thick and twisting trunk, which will have a rhythm similar to the serpent's coils. Everything working together in harmony. Just like in one of his favourite stories from Chrétien de Troyes. A wandering knight comes to an enchanted place and sees rising before him a single tree where many birds have come to perch and sing, and their different songs all come together to make one song. The verses sound in his head and bring him some peace.

In spite of the spring weather, it is still cold in the long, narrow room where the monks sit hunched over their manuscripts. The scratching of their pens and the scraping of penknife against quill mingles with the creaking of their chairs and from time to time a cough, a clearing of the throat. Ah, if he could see Eloise now, if he could ride up the road to her and tell her what happened. But then, wouldn't she go pale and cry out and turn away from him? The story that now torments him is not a story from his pilgrimage to the holy land, not a story to be told by the family fire while showing off a sunburned face and tanned feet. Not a story of deserts and ships and seabirds or something silly like the description of a bouquet of violets bought on impulse in the marketplace in Damascus.

No, he would have to kneel at her feet and say, Eloise, I have killed a human brother, I have stabbed him and left him dead on the forest floor. Eloise, the demons will come for me when I die and the hellfires will devour me forever.

John concentrates on the images to come and thinks about how he will place Adam and Eve on the page, and later, how he will do the ark with all its windows or the whale vomiting Jonah out onto the dry land. His lips move as he slowly outlines another scale with his fine brush, half praying, half repeating to himself that he is a painter, not a murderer, that he is of noble blood, younger brother to the lord Baudoin, an accomplished traveller, an illuminator of manuscripts, and, above all, a master of the fresco.

There had been two of them. It had happened at the end of a day of hunting. His brother had urged him to delay his departure. "Stay! It will be a fine day," Baudoin had said. "Stay! Stay!"

The day had been all that Baudoin had promised, and John had lingered in the forest after the stag had gone down and the baying of the bloodhounds had faded into the distance. He had slowed his horse to a walk, enjoying the glimmering of the sun on the leaves and the first smells of spring. He had dismounted and taken a few steps toward a clump of bushes to relieve himself when suddenly they were on him. Later he realised they must have jumped down out of a tree. He was flung to the ground and his arms were jerked back. He felt a knee between his shoulder blades and a blow to the side of his head. But the blow had lacked heft, and with a twist he had shaken off his assailants and leapt to his feet. They were young, scarcely more than boys, and they stood there half crouched before him, looking for a way to pounce. They were incredibly filthy. John had begun to speak when the first boy threw himself at him like a raging cat. He hung at John's neck, trying to bite, kicking, one hand feeling for a purse, a clasp, anything. John succeeded in pushing him off again. But now he drew the long hunting knife from his belt. When they both rushed at him again, desperately, he struck and one of the boys fell to the ground. With a shout, the other dashed away and disappeared between the trees. John had knelt down beside the filthy boy.

"Hungry, so tired," the young man had mumbled just before he died.

After John confessed to old Bernard, the priest

had said to him in his blunt way, "Go to the monks down the valley from Rochefort. Pray there, and be useful to them. Make a confession to the abbot, Father Martin, and then do as he advises you."

Perhaps, after a while, he can reveal to the monks the extent of his talents. He will follow the rule, keep to the discipline, and perhaps they will let him work in their new chapel. The high rounded rise of the apse behind the altar, the crypt below, all those walls are still bare. One day he had dared to mention this to the abbot, in the cloister where talking was allowed. Father Martin was a tall, solemn-faced man with a long scar running from eyebrow to chin. He had not replied. Still, his eyes had seemed kind. He had nodded, signifying understanding. John can envision the work, all the images he could paint, King David with his harp, Cain and Abel, the Virgin with gentle hands. And up in the light behind the altar, the wide gaze of the Christ. He is good at his art, he is a master too now, perhaps even better than the Greek. And he longs to be at his trade once again, working quickly as one must, applying line and colour to the moist surface before it dries. Perhaps he had killed a man, but if he paints well, could that not be counted as retribution? The tall abbot had said nothing when he asked about the chapel, but his slight nod had meant that he understood the need of a painter to paint. And John had known in the same instant that this monk who had surely experienced war must himself be a man in sympathy now with some kind of work.

Night has fallen and John lies on his narrow bed in the dormitory, grateful for the locked gates, grateful for the oil lamp kept burning in one window. Perhaps he will be able to speak again with the kind-eyed abbot. The man must have been a fighter in his youth, with such a scar. As John slips into sleep, his last thoughts are of the upcurving white walls waiting for his touch.

DARK IS A TIME OF DANGER AND ELOISE KNOWS IT as everyone does. Lights must be left burning to keep evil away. Like the monks, she too must always have a light burning in the room. From its niche in the wall, it flickers in the night breeze. She can just make out the falcon lady riding on in the coloured threads of the tapestry. Beside her in the bed, Robert seems lost in sleep. Eloise watches the flickering flame, her knees pulled up against her chest, her joined hands flat under her cheek.

"Look here to me, my lady," Robert had said to her at the evening meal. "Look, I have brought you music and song."

Then she saw a young man rising from the fireside at her husband's beckoning gesture. He walked forward, tall, with a slight stoop to his shoulders.

"Play and sing for us now," Robert had ordered, with no preamble, no exchange of banter with the singer, and Eloise had caught the shock on her sister's face at this lack of manners.

The trobar had lowered his head and the little clown had come skipping forward with a bench. Everyone was still smiling from his antics, but now the little fellow sat down beside the trobar and pulled a wooden flute from the pouch he carried slung around his shoulders. In a low voice, the trobar announced his song.

Both sat still for a moment and then the juggler, tapping a slow rhythm on the floor, raised the flute to his lips. The piercing notes flew up and up into the rafters until a lower strumming from the harp brought them down and then the singer's voice filled the room.

As the song story of Tristan and Isolde unfolded itself to Eloise, as the rhythm took hold and the familiar images arose before her eyes, she felt as if she were seeing long-lost landscapes, a beloved country, and she walked into it with sure and eager steps. Soon she was outside herself. Although she had not looked into the singer's face, soon she was walking beside him and it seemed to her that she was Isolde and that the singer had turned into the moving form of Tristan. Soon they were together in the heat on the deck of the ship and she felt her hand taking the cup from his hand and together they drank the potion and the enchanted liquid went into their veins. And when the wind filled the sails, hurrying them to the king, they could no longer bear to be apart.

In the night-darkened room, up on her stool by the window, Eloise presses her forehead against the cool stone wall. As the trobar had sung the last verses of the evening, she had lifted her eyes to his, catching a glimpse of grey-green and a hawk nose before looking quickly away. And in an instant she had known him.

ROBERT TURNS IN THE BED. SHE HAS MOVED AWAY from him again. He knows, without opening his eyes, that she sits by the window, motionless. Robert keeps his breathing deep and slow. He does not like the singer. Because the singer, this wanderer, this good-for-nothing warbler, has brought the light back into her eyes, the light that he has been watching for, waiting for, the light that he so loved to see.

DOWN IN THE LITTLE GARDEN, THE FRUIT TREES ARE in full bloom, the three apple, the two pear. Eloise sits on a stone bench, bending slightly forward as she threads her needle with green. Her sister plays in the grass with the child. Suddenly Eloise cannot see and her tears fall onto the pattern of leaves, making them darker. The wind blows and blossoms swirl and fall onto the grass all around her.

"The trobar should not have looked so long into your eyes," murmurs her sister. "And you should not have allowed it. That was not courteous and, for your husband, a great insult."

On the second evening she had walked away with him once more into the story. She had kept her eyes down, she had kept her eyes on her clasped hands, on the folds of her dress, on the shine of her belt of silver and leather. But all the same she had been with him. As soon as he had begun she had stepped out of herself and followed. She was seated beside her husband in the flickering candlelight, but she travelled with the trobar, she was young and free, walking beside him through the story, feeling the heat of the sun, seeing the moon rise and the stars twinkling, plunging into the deep dark forest, sailing over the gleaming sea.

And as he sang, Thomas knew that she walked beside him in the story, as surely as he could hear her little voice calling, over and over, from somewhere up high out of the stone.

On the third evening he had begun another song,

one that spoke of such love for a lady that winter cold seemed to become a blossoming tree and white snow unfolding leaves of green. And her eyes had lifted to his and they had stared at each other in wonder and in shameless recognition.

What wild beast had sobbed then from Robert's throat as he leapt from his chair at her side and vaulted over the table. In an instant the harp had been flung across the floor into the shadows, and the man of arms had the singer by the throat. He had struck him across the forehead, and blood had come running down the trobar's face and streamed into his hair. Robert's fingers tightened around the singer's neck. He knew he could kill him very easily right here on the stone floor, and he wanted to kill him for staring into the girl's eyes. But looking down into the young man's face he saw with surprise that the trobar had no fear of him. The trobar had in his gaze what Robert had learned to value in his companions, in those he chose for the wars. And so he pushed the singer aside with a curse and still on his knees and short of breath he cursed again and turned away, saying, "You will leave at once. There will be the things I promised, but you will leave."

She knew Merle would come walking that night, she waited for her slow, steady steps, her low humming, and her hands, hovering, then lightly touching the bedcovers over their bodies, flitting across their faces like the silvery fish in the river at home. Merle stood very still for a long time next to Robert's side of the bed before moving away, pushing the curtain, crossing the big round room and going to her alcove on the other side.

IN THE MONASTERY, JOHN IS DREAMING. HE SLEEPS on his cot alongside the monks and dreams. In his dream he sees a strange beast. It has long silken fur and seems to be a very large dog, but thin and weak. The animal struggles, trying to get up. The long fur on its skinny ribcage glistens and rolls. Still the creature remains on the ground. Finally it lowers its head onto its front paws and sighs. John comes out of his dream. The fear grips him at once. He pushes it away with thoughts of the monks and their prayers going up and up day and night. Does this not protect him, is he not safe from harm?

Matins, lauds, prime, terce, sext, none, vespers, compline.

JOHN DRIFTS OFF AGAIN AND ANOTHER DREAM begins. Lightning flashes across the sky and a devil leers in his face, blue with pointed teeth. And behind the blue devil, in the underbrush, a wolf lurks, waiting for him. He hears its low growl. John stirs in his sleep; a faint sigh rises from his lips.

OUT IN THE DARKNESS, BABEL STAMPS ALONG behind his trobar and grumbles about all that had been promised them and that they now leave behind as if they were noble lords in need of nothing, as if they had the means to be great givers throwing gold into the wind. Thomas lets him talk. He does not reply and he does not slow his pace. At the edge of the forest bordering the monastery Thomas pushes their last coins into Babel's hands.

"Go on alone now," he says to the juggler. "I cannot tell you when I will join you."

"Have you gone mad?" Babel dares to ask.

"Perhaps," answers Thomas, and without another word he turns away and disappears into the shadows between the trees.

JOHN OPENS HIS EYES AGAIN. FAINT LIGHT SHOWS AT the windows. Better to remain awake, he says to himself. Better to try to remember good things. The gypsies singing in that distant valley when he was on his way home to France. Their women kneeling by the wide river, rinsing out the newly dyed cloth in the swift water, red, green, and blue swirling out into the stream. The light increases. Better to think about his Andalusian woman, yes, the one who travelled with him for a time, and her soft skin and the bracelets she wore on her ankles and the jewels in her ears.

UP AT THE FORTRESS, THE PROMISED HORSES STRAIN at their leads in the stables. No one has come to fetch them and the trobar has gone.

A shepherd and his wife have begun the shearing of the sheep. They grab the struggling, bleating animals by their hind legs and pull them down across their laps. They slice the wool away from the warm bodies in swaths with their shears.

In the wheatfields, a woman is sharpening her scythe with a stone.

ROBERT RAISES HIS ARMS AND THE BOY SLIDES THE coat of mail down over his shoulders. The familiar weight reassures him and he swears to keep this good feeling close. He needs it to preserve his strength, his quick eye. He will think only good thoughts now. He will remember the time they made him one of theirs. Right on the battlefield, his wound still running with blood. He will feel again the heavy slap to the back of his neck from Baudoin's hand and hear the low murmur of admiration and approval going around the circle of men.

This is the best feeling. It runs through him in a

wave of heat down to his fingertips. The boy lowers the helmet onto his head and Robert feels the skirt of chain mail crumple slightly at his shoulders. One foot into the stirrup and he is up, his men all rising onto their mounts as well, swirling and shouting and clattering around him. Spirits are high, they are off to be part of the great lord's team in an important tournament, the biggest one of the summer. He will win for Baudoin, he will take prisoners as winners do in the games and ransom them off and return richer than when he left.

New tools are needed for the fields, new weapons for the hunt and blankets for the winter, and seed. He should have killed the damned singer, snapped his wretched neck right there on the floor. But no matter. The miserable fellow is gone. Gone, he repeats to himself, gone, gone, and never to return. The gates to the fortress are swinging open. Robert puts the spurs to his horse and the beast trembles and starts forward. He rides out and his men follow him.

Cornflowers and poppies bloom in the wheatfields between the ripe stalks. Backs are bending, arms and scythes are moving down and around, down and around. A woman follows the reapers down the furrows, gathering the fallen grain and tying it up in sheaves.

In July, the night is eight hours long, the day sixteen.

ELOISE SITS IN THE GARDEN UNDER THE STIRRING leaves, their shadows tremble on her dress, on the grass. Fruit has begun to swell on the branches, weighing them down, red apples, yellow pears. She sees the trobar's hand on the strings of his harp. She brings the image back into her mind's eye over and over and it feels like the water rushing up out of the mountain springs. Her sister calls to her, saying something about little John, how he reaches for the toy horse on wheels, how he laughs, but Eloise is not listening.

In the nights, as the weeks pass, she knows that he has not gone away. She senses that he is near, somewhere in the forest, perhaps sleeping on a bed of pine branches at night and waiting through the long summer days. Over and over she remembers how she first heard the harp sounds, how they mingled with the stamping of the horses from below and how all the food smells made her feel ill once she had seen him, once his voice had come over her, once her eyes had rested in his gaze.

The air had been heavy all day and now a thunderstorm rumbles in the distance. There will be rain before morning. Robert is far away, at the tournament, at the jousting, and she feels a wringing of her conscience and turns in the bed. Sleep comes. But soon she awakens again. The candle has gone out. It has rained, she can smell it, but now the rain has stopped. She creeps to the window, to her place on the high stool. And then she hears. Far away. From somewhere in the forest, the trobar's voice, faintly rising and falling. After a time, she can make out the words:

Lady in your garden,
wait for the hour
when only stars shine.

Eloise repeats the words in a whisper. She sits at her window until the first birds begin to sing.

Above the chapel doorway, there is a sculpted stone image of Eve. Wide-eyed, curious and apprehensive, in the first light of dawn, she seems to be floating forward breathlessly between dancing trees, yet she is reaching back behind her with one hand to pluck the fruit.

In August, the night is ten hours long, the day fourteen.

WILLIAM IS WALKING IN THE FOREST. THERE IS A LOAF of bread in his shoulder bag. From time to time Father Martin from the monastery climbs up here and leaves some food in the hut. William strides along, disappearing between the trees with his long staff and his bag. The sun is not yet up, but the hermit senses that the young man will soon be gone, and quickens his pace.

When he stumbled onto the fellow for the first time, William had been alone for so long that he had felt a shock at the sight of another human being. He had almost tripped over him, a ragged, curly-headed boy sleeping on the edge of a clearing on a bed of pine boughs, his lips stained with the juices from wild berries. William had rasped and coughed, his voice hoarse from lack of use, before being able to speak.

"Foolish," he had croaked. "Foolish boy to sleep out in the open. Bears ... wolves ..."

Then he had watched the young man wake up and had given him an apple.

Now they sit, face to face, on the ground. Thomas chews at the bread, bone weary. Yet he feels full of light.

"You are going soon," says the hermit.

Thomas is grateful to the old man, he would like to tell him what has happened to him, but he only replies, "Yes, I must go."

The hermit keeps on studying Thomas, taking in this undefined something about the boy, absorbing it for his prayers.

AS SOON AS THOMAS HAD LOOKED INTO HER EYES, they had come together out of the long ago, out of that childhood place in the dark before day. And now he is changed because she lives in him. For her he has made words and music come together, he has made something not learned by heart. And it feels as if he had pulled a clear fire out of the snow.

Thomas stands up. He thanks the holy man and they remain standing together for a time without speaking. Then the hermit blesses him and Thomas shoulders his pack and goes.

WILLIAM WATCHES THE BOY'S LEAN FIGURE UNTIL HE can no longer see anything moving between the trees. Sometimes he wonders whether he is still a man or become simply another creature of the forest. Perhaps, except for Father Martin, the scar-faced abbot, they have forgotten him down in the monastery. He doesn't go there anymore, preferring to pray alone under the sky and the trees, preferring the breathing of the wind and the sudden appearances of deer. He raises his face to receive the coming of the light.

DOWN BY THE RIVERBANK THE WORK ON THE MILL is going well and Father Martin is pleased. Soon the wheat from their fields will be ground into flour here. The river water will be redirected to flow down onto the paddles of the wheel from a flume and send them rolling around the drive shaft and this motion will be transferred through the wheeling gears inside the mill and set the millstones to grinding, one remaining steady, the one that is called the sleeping stone, the other one going around and around, crushing the grain, grinding it into flour for bread. The workmen hammer and saw. A heavyset fellow is rolling one of the massive millstones along the riverbank. Martin strides forward to help with the pushing.

In a field, women with white kerchiefs tied around their heads are raking hay. One stops to stretch. The wooden handle of the pitch-fork resting against one shoulder, she places her hands behind her hips and leans back on them slowly, then wipes the sweat from her fore-head with her sleeve. Now she grasps her pitchfork and goes back to work. The air is filled with the steady stridulation of the crickets.

THE BEGGAR LOOKS LIKE AN OLD MAN. HIS CLOTHES are covered with dust, and a hood hides his bearded face. He has appeared out of nowhere. He sits in the sunlight near the kitchens, his dusty hand trembling as he extends it to beg.

The cook looks hard at the fellow and then, wiping her hands on her apron, disappears into the kitchen. She emerges with a bowl of lentils, a slab of bread, and a jug of water from the well. The shabby fellow eats, dipping the bread into the lentils and taking long drafts from the water jug. When he sees the cook again, he asks if he might sleep for a while in the stables. The old woman nods and the beggar hobbles away and disappears.

But once into the shadows the man's body straightens and he climbs quickly and easily up into the loft and buries himself behind the hay. The brightest hours pass, and since no one sees him again and because few people noticed him coming up the road at such an early hour, his presence is forgotten.

On the wild and rocky plain above Rochefort, all through the afternoon, the bees hum and the blue-green pines bend and sigh and the clouds come boiling up over the mountains and roll their way across the sky, trailing their shadows over the windswept land.

ELOISE BENDS DOWN IN THE DARK AND PULLS ON her shoes. Night has fallen and the fortress sleeps. Tonight there is no moon in the sky, only stars. It is time. Drawing a cloak around her shoulders, she gets up and pads silently out of the room. She is no more than a shadow slipping down the winding steps, into the courtyard, past the chapel, no more than a grey flickering against the stone as she slips into the little garden and slides into the deeper darkness under the branches of the largest apple tree.

Now he is nearing, now he is kneeling at her side, and their hands touch.

"Lady," he whispers.

"Thomas," she answers.

Now time is gentle with them. It passes slowly. Perhaps it stops.

"I could see your hands, I remember your hands in front of the flames when you were a boy."

And he answers by lifting her fingers to his cheek. Now they lean together under the tree and their lips touch and press and then they are gone. The tree rustles over them, but they are no longer in the world. Between undressing and dressing their bodies are like smooth silver moving on the grass until the returning light makes them flesh again.

When full day comes, the garden is empty and the stone bench is very white.

IT HAS BEGUN TO RAIN. ELOISE WORKS AT HER sewing, pushing her needle up and down through the cloth, pulling the red and white beads into place, making a flower. Thunder sounds in the distance. Sheep are grazing in the field below. A bell is ringing the hour.

Merle has come into the room and, plodding forward, she stops just behind Eloise, and stands there, not speaking.

After a time she says, "There was a beggar."

Eloise does not reply. And then, quietly, "Come,

give me your hand. Come feel the pattern of flowers I am sewing onto this belt."

She reaches back for Merle's hand and runs the older woman's fingers over the embroidery.

"Can you feel them? Some are large, full open, and some are tiny buds. They are red and white, with the green leaves between them. I wish you could see the work."

Merle allows her hand to be guided, she makes no effort to pull away.

"There was a beggar here yesterday," she repeats tonelessly. "And before that, someone sang in the night."

"A beggar?" answers Eloise, her heart pounding fast. "How should I know about a beggar? They come and we feed them and they go. Sit beside me now, we will sing something together while I work."

Merle takes her place beside Eloise on the bench, keeping her hand on the girl's arm. Eloise gives her arm a little shake.

"Can you take your hand away now, it makes the work difficult."

"This beggar has not gone," says the woman doggedly.

Eloise hears her voice rising as she replies, "Let us not worry about a poor beggar. No harm can come from a beggar."

And she removes Merle's hand firmly from her arm.

"Some harm perhaps," comes the answer. "Some harm and perhaps even much harm. You should tell him to go away."

"I? I?" breathes Eloise.

The rain has stopped and the sky has begun to clear. Suddenly sunlight streams over their hands. The young girl's moving deftly, the older woman's heavy, loosely joined in her lap. Eloise keeps silent. Outside the birds have resumed their chirping.

Finally she whispers, "He will soon be gone."

And Merle replies to her softly, "Then all will be well."

A stag has fallen into a trap set by a ploughman. The animal struggles down in the hole, his forelegs caught in a web of ropes. He rears up, he throws his crowned head back and back, repeatedly.

In August, the night is ten hours long, the day fourteen.

THE NIGHT AT LAST. NO SHOES, NO CLOTHES, ONLY the long cape. Down the stairs as in a dream and into the garden. Only an instant to wait and he is there and they come together with a little cry. And the shadows swallow them, clinging to each other and whispering, sinking, mouth to mouth.

Later the wind stirs suddenly, restlessly through the leaves over their heads, and then they hear a sound.

"Hush," she says. "Listen." In an instant she knows. Merle is walking in the garden, her skirt is trailing on the grass. Up and down she walks with her low humming. And then, just as suddenly, after another gust of wind, she is gone.

A shout sounds from outside the tower walls. The men have returned. Robert has come home. A last look, a last kiss, mouth to mouth, and they tear apart. Running for the stairway, Eloise realises with a shock that Merle has warned her. Why? Why? Up and around, up and around she runs. Quick, the little bottle of rosewater, her smell. Quick, to douse herself, to throw off the scent that covers her. Scattering, trembling, the drops run down all over her body and she rubs them into her skin, harder and harder, breasts, belly and between her legs, arms, neck, fingertips, and feet. The cloak flung over a trunk, she leaps into the bed. "Quiet, heart!" she commands herself. "Sleep, sleep, to be asleep." She repeats the chant, sleep, sleep, to be asleep. Now she hears his step, the sound of his boots on the stairs, crossing the big round room toward the heavy curtain that still separates them. A weary step, she guesses. Good. A weary step. Her hands are too hot. She rubs them against the covers, pushes them against the wall. The boy must be with him, to help him undress. Perhaps the boy will stay and sleep at the foot of the bed. No, as he pushes the curtain aside she knows there is no boy, only Robert, bone weary, only Robert pulling off his clothes alone.

"Your rose smell," he murmurs, lying beside her. "Lovely rose smell." There will be no getting away from this. Closer, closer, praying to the Virgin and all the saints he notices nothing. Closer and closer until he can be no closer.

"My rose," he whispers, "my rose."

THOMAS IS RUNNING. THIS IS THE END. HIS HEART is breaking in his breast, he can feel it bleeding. He wants to die in the forest, to have his grave at her feet. To cleave to the trees, to become a rustling that she can hear. To be a little wind near her ear. To be a little wind at the back of her neck. To be a little pearl between her fingers. A mote of dust in a shaft of sun settling on her shoulder. He has slipped out between the weary horsemen, hobbling and lurching like a drunken boat, a silhouette of madness and age, and they let him pass without a murmur or a glance.

IN THE DARKNESS AT THE TOP OF THE TOWER, A SMILE flits over Merle's lips. The beggar is going, the beggar has gone. She listens. Robert is in his rightful place. She has kept the peace. She has seen to that. No shouting, no anger, no pain. His bed creaks from behind the heavy curtain. She hears him groan and sigh. All is well. He holds the land, he wields a sword, he has a son, her plan has worked, she has succeeded. And now the forest people come to whisper to her as they often do just before she falls asleep, flowing and streaming around her head in circles, then whirling slowly, slowly away, back to the river and back to the trees.

At the bottom of the trap, the stag lies still, eyes glazed over, an arrow in his heart. Men are coming quickly through the dusk with hooks and ropes to haul him up.

EVERYONE IS GOING ON THE HUNT TODAY. ALL THE guests Robert has brought back from the games, barons and their ladies from the valleys around, and Eloise must go too. She must go with them all and ride the dapple grey that Robert has given her.

"A gentle beast, lady, you will see," he says, looking at her with happy eyes.

Her hair neatly braided, she is dressed in green. She sits on the wide back of the dapple grey, her long sleeves lined in red silk trailing down. The day is fine and everyone is talking and laughing. Bodies sway from side to side, leather creaks and bridles clink as the hunting party crosses a fallow field heading toward the line of trees on the other side. The valets are walking ahead of the group, thumping the ground with their long sticks and holding back their bloodhounds.

Soon they will disappear into the trees to find the scent of the boar, a large male who has been getting into the vineyards, and when they have it and the hunting horn sounds, the kennel master will go in behind them with the other dogs and the men will put the spurs to their mounts and leap forward.

She wears the belt of red and white roses.

Hoes are chopping down in the adjacent field, hands are pulling up weeds, row after row. The peasants whisper to each other about the stag, the good venison they will have, and how the hole was quickly filled and no one the wiser.

A CROW CAWS FROM A TREETOP. SHE SWAYS WITH THE movement of the grey, she closes her eyes. She does not want to see the day.

Suddenly one of the valets surprises a hare. It leaps up and away and begins darting across the field in spurts of speed, right and left in a zigzag fashion. The men and women burst out laughing; they begin to applaud the little animal.

Robert looks back at Eloise, who is now watching

the frightened beast, her eyes widening. On impulse, as a lighthearted joke, he puts the spurs to his horse and takes off after the flying creature. This is his day, this is his glorious return home. He looks back at her once more and she smiles on him as she must. With another thrust, both spurs to the flanks, he is at a gallop. Releasing the reins, stretching high in the saddle, he raises his lance in the midst of loud laughter and louder applause. But the horse stumbles at full speed, a sharp crack echoes back and Robert is thrown forward onto the ground. A sigh soars up from the riders like a sudden gust of wind and then Eloise is pushing forward with the others. Somehow she finds herself on her knees in the dirt and weeds beside him. One of his men is holding Robert's bleeding head, all twisted away in a strange position.

"God have mercy on my soul," he mumbles, "for my body has come to an end."

Bending over him, her lips close to his ear, she whispers, "Robert, Robert."

Her voice seems to be coming from outside herself. She straightens and sees her husband looking up, he has heard her voice. The blood is draining from his face, his face is white as new-fallen snow.

He says, "I cannot see you, lady. Where are you?"

"I am here, I am here beside you," she cries. The

crow caws raucously from the forest. Robert's lips move again, but there is no sound.

JOHN STANDS ON THE SCAFFOLDING BEHIND THE altar. They have trusted him, they have given him the work. The concave surface is moist, all is ready. Dipping his brush into the dark red colour he outlines the head, the neck, the beginning of the shoulders, the arms. Now the eyes, wide-set, steady and compassionate, eyes that pardon. And now the lips that speak forgiveness. Quickly the colour for the half-parted lips, for the good dark eyes. They look back at him, glistening from the wall. His hand is steady and his eye is keen. He is bringing the whole figure up out of the wall, gleaming, the hand raised to bless, the wide breast. Soon he will be bringing out the angels, he can paint many angels today, he can go on and on.

THE MEN HAVE MANAGED TO CREATE A STRETCHER with two lances and a thick cape. Now they are carrying Robert across the field in the direction of the fortress. Eloise walks behind them, stumbling on her dress. She falls and picks herself up, walks on and stumbles again. On the periphery of her vision, the dapple grey is cantering away, the little silver bells on his bridle jingling.

Strange sounds are coming from her throat, her breathing is shallow. Though her eyes are blurred with tears, she sees a tall, dark figure looming at the edge of the road leading up to the fortress gates, looming and waiting, somehow knowing. The sun is high in the sky. Merle's hand closes around her arm. Without a word and never loosening her hold she walks up the road beside Eloise behind the makeshift stretcher. Like the first day they met, being led, yet leading.

In the long hall, someone rushes for one of the long boards and the trestles to set up a table. His men lift Robert up and they lay him gently out on the worn wooden surface.

JOHN GOES ON WORKING. RED, RED, DARK REDDISH brown, the colour of oxblood. Now green again, green, sliding down the white plaster at the edge of the wall. A bright flash distracts him. He hears the clattering of wooden shoes. The monks' pupils, the young schol-ars are passing under the windows of the chapel, doing their chores, some carrying water from the well, some lugging wood. The water in their buckets has caught the sun and its reflection has been thrown up quiver-ing onto the ceiling. They speak more softly as they go by as if remembering some order from the brothers. John smiles. But then a few words reach his ears from their high voices. "The baron Robert ... fallen ... dying ..."

John's hand continues to move. Red, red, close to the white, making it bright, then green and wider green. Suddenly the rocky coast of Catalunya rises before his eyes, the way to the south, to the port of Barcelona. He sees the shining sea, he hears the wind, he smells the gusts of wild rosemary under the hot sun. He must go to her. He must leave his sanctuary and go to her.

The grapes have been harvested in Robert's vineyards. A barefoot man is trampling them in the vat, up to his knees in the fruit. The juice has begun to flow down a runnel, the mother drops, the juice that comes from the very first pressure and will make the best wine.

FATHER MARTIN IS PRAYING. ROBERT'S MEN ARE kneeling all around him, a crown of men around their lord. All are watching for the moment when his soul will leave his body, all hope for a sight of this. Eloise kneels, farther away, with Merle and the other women, Flora and the servants behind them. Robert has been given no dying time, no time for last words to his companions, to his little son. No time to be dressed in monk's robes as he had wished, no time to give away his possessions in order to leave this world with nothing but his soul. No time, no time. Eloise feels as if the crow she heard in the field were pecking at her heart. She moans. Bright spots come dancing before her eyes and she falls into the dark.

Robert is in a harbour, he senses the movement of the ship under his feet. When he returns from Jerusalem he will have a statue made for his tomb. It will be a likeness of himself with helmet and coat of mail and sword and glove. In the lapping waters along the bow he sees the turn of her head, he hears her voice. In the hall where he lies on the table his lips form her name. Now they are pulling out of the harbour, the sails billow out, and his gloved fist closes around the handle of his sword. She was very young. He can feel the salt spray in his beard. The taste of it is on his tongue. She was hardly more than a child. His coat of mail scrapes against the wood. The ship moves out into the open sea. A young man is standing just behind him, tall and strong, his little son all grown, his heir, his bloodline. Together they will become like the hawk as it soars down on the thrush. They will take back the holy city. They will plunge into wonders.

One of Robert's men has knelt down beside her. He is speaking. She does not want to hear what he is saying, but the meaning of his words reaches her at last.

"Lady, he is gone from this world."

The ploughman whistles at the oxen and they move forward, pulling the harrow along the furrows. A big stone weighs the harrow down, its wooden teeth penetrate the newly ploughed soil, break up the last clods and push the seed for the winter wheat well down into the earth. A few magpies have gathered at the edge of the field. They peck at the ground and fly up again with their raucous calls.

On the far side of the field where the harrowing has been completed, a woman is bending over, reaching for something that is lying on the ground. She lifts a scarecrow, a cloth man stuffed with straw, nailed to a pole, and holding a crude bow. Stepping forward carefully, the scarecrow balanced over her head, she plunges the pointed stake of the straw man into the ground, pushing down on it with all of her weight. Now she pulls a few thin rods of wood from a pouch at her waist and begins pushing them into the ground as well at regular intervals between the planted furrows. Bending over the last one, she reaches into her pouch again and takes out a ball of string. Knotting one end around the stick and moving and knotting from stick to stick, she slowly creates a zigzag pattern of string over the field.

When the harrowing is done and all the string is strung, the man and the woman go home. Now the scarecrow stands alone with his bow over the web of string. The web shines white in the last light of day. The magpies call from the surrounding trees until nightfall.

Matins, lauds, prime, terce, sext, none, vespers, compline.
Matins, lauds, prime, terce, sext, none, vespers, compline.

In September, the night is twelve hours long, the day twelve.
In October, the night is fourteen hours long, the day ten.

THOMAS STUMBLES THROUGH THE UNDERBRUSH, wanting to get deeper into the forest, to hide, to roll into the earth, perhaps even to become a forest man like the hermit and live alone in prayer from sun to sun to sun. As he crosses a small clearing, he trips on a vine and falls, knocking his head against a jutting root. Opening his eyes, he finds himself face to face with a little grass snake, rolled up in the sun. Thomas stares into its motionless golden eyes. It is warm in the clearing. He pushes himself slowly backwards. The cicadas are whirring. Now his head is resting on the ground. The snake has not moved. Thomas feels that the snake has accepted him. He closes his eyes and, in spite of the throbbing on his forehead, welcomes the heat of the sun as it penetrates his clothing and warms his back and his legs. Something is hovering around him, just barely out of reach, a perfume, a presence, someone trying to speak. Or is it his own voice? How many days has he been without food and water? His own voice, his own self, reaching for her in the garden? Just before falling asleep, Thomas remembers how it felt, the first time he managed to make a sound, the first clear, high note coming out of the flute from his lips and from his breath.

SHE IS PALE AND WEAK, SHE FEELS LIKE STONE. SHE doesn't care. Someone is crossing the big round room, someone who is looking for her. She hears Flora's voice, speaking low, and her sisters' too, both Hedwige and Eleanor, murmuring, conferring quickly about something. She doesn't care. Her hands lie idle in her lap. No sewing, no embroidery, no cutting and piecing, no spinning, nothing for these hands. Nothing. She wants to die.

The curtain moves, is pushed aside, and a man comes in. She lifts her head and stares at him. He is older, bearded, but the eyes are the same.

"Uncle John," she whispers.

John crosses the room quickly, kneels down beside her, and takes her hand.

"My Eloise, how is it with you?"

"How can you be here?" she murmurs in wonder, forgetting her torment for an instant.

"I am," he answers simply. "They say my brother has sent for you, for you and the child."

She looks at him without a word and the two of them remain face to face, hand in hand, motionless in the quiet room, Eloise sitting in her chair, John kneeling before her. All around them, from tile to tile, the little red fox stops and runs, stops and runs. Up on the wall, the falcon lady rides, leaning slightly forward as if she had just agreed to something, the fierce bird on her wrist.

John takes Eloise into his arms, pulling her from her chair. Now they are both kneeling on the floor. He holds her tight, rocks her gently back and forth, kisses her neatly braided hair, her pale cheeks. Her head pressed against his shoulder, she begins to shudder and the tears come at last and she sobs in her uncle's embrace.

As the sun sinks behind the mountain, she finds the words to tell him.

And just before full dark he, in turn, tells her about the day of hunting and the wretched boy.

The oil lamps burn from their little alcoves.

"Pilgrims," he says, taking her hands once more into his.

"My uncle?"

"Pilgrims," he repeats. "Yes. You and I. We shall be pilgrims. Father Martin has told me to go. And you must come with me. We will make the voyage together. First south to San Pere de Rodes, then west to Saint Jacques de Compostelle. I will care for you. I will show you the bright sea. And we will both find our pardon."

He lifts her hands to his lips, kisses both palms, and then places them gently back into her lap.

It is noon. The day is bright. A freshly cut gravestone has been fitted into the floor of the monastery church. Nearby, a sculptor is standing on a scaffolding. He is working on the figures of three young men at the top of a column. They have joined arms. Their hands and legs are turning into vines and leaves. The sculptor whistles as he chisels and taps his finishing touches. He can feel his whistling going into the dancing tendrils and leaves.

SHE RIDES BEHIND HIM UNDER THE RAIN. IT IS A light summer rain. Little droplets are catching in her hair and making a silvery web on her woolen cape. The child, her son, is safe with her mother, and she rides south, a pilgrim. Going toward the light that will save her and make her whole again. Going. Both of them.

She sees Robert's parched lips forming her name. She sees her hands going into Thomas's hands. She feels again the hours and the days, how they lived in hiding, rolled into themselves, waiting for the return of night. She feels herself as she was, breathing lightly over her sewing, her whole body like a cloud, feels how she made it rise and float through the walls and into his body, waiting for her under the hay, and watching, watching, hour after hour, for the waning of the light. She feels his lips on her neck and the grass under their backs in the garden. She smells the weeds and the blood as she knelt over her fallen husband.

John looks back at Eloise. She smiles. He feels at peace. He will be able to care for her for a while. He leads, he ministers, he is on a good road. He has had another dream of the strange dog. But in this dream, the animal had fattened and gained strength. In this new dream, the beast had risen easily to its feet and, shaking out its shining fur, had ambled away, indifferent and free.

As in the dream, John feels his own limbs loosening, his heart lightening. They are riding along a high, rocky trail. The rain has stopped. Eloise pushes at her hood and it falls back onto her shoulders. The sun is shining and she turns with a thrill to look out again over the bright, endlessly moving sea. The smell of wild rosemary wafts past them from time to time, and the wind gusts at their backs.

THE FOREST PEOPLE ARE COMING, SLIDING DOWN from the sky, from the high clouds where they have been whirling together. They come right down through the stone as if it were made of air, and they circle slowly around her head, whispering, *Merle, Merle*, their fingers trailing over her body, over her eyes and lips. They slip down between her clothes, cooling her, cleansing her, and telling her to stand up and to walk, to come with them, come with them down to the water.

No one stops her. Not a servant, not a horseman, not an apprentice. Perhaps they do not see her.

"I am coming, I am coming, I am the blackbird," she whispers as she goes down the river path with steady steps. They are chanting inside her head now, they are coursing inside her body and she is as one with them. If she spreads her arms wide, she will rise up into the air and whirl and soar and dive with them.

The more she succeeded with her son, the more they took away her light. And when he had become a baron at last, when he had returned and taken her up from the village and put her in the tower with the keys at her waist and orders on her lips, her darkness had become complete.

Now they have punished her enough for leaving them, for turning away from them. Is she not of the trees, born from the trees, and are they not her people, her own? They want to take her back, they call and call and call. They are waiting for her in the water and the air, and water and air are the same. It will be like the times with Anselme, in the place where the river ran smooth when, at the end of the day, the swallows would come swooping down in wide curves, their wings whispering over the flow, just grazing, barely touching the surface, and leaving a tiny ripple before rising fast again and wheeling up into the sky.

A little fox watches from the riverbank. He blinks, his vertical pupils black in his shining yellow eyes. His bushy tail twitches back and forth as he keeps his gaze fixed on the tall human creature walking into the river. For an instant the cold has made the creature hesitate, but she pushes forward again, opens her arms, and now the water is rushing and rising around her waist. Suddenly she sinks to her knees and bends away with the pull of the current. As she passes the mill where the great round stones turn against each other's massive faces, her sight comes back and she goes down toward the shimmering hands.

A monk picks up a delicate leaf of gold, holding it carefully between thumb and forefinger. His hand hovers for an instant over the page; now he lowers the quivering little square and presses it firmly against the design. Good. The leaf is adhering properly. Using a soft brush, he detaches the fragments not captured by the glue. Slowly the intricate form of the letter appears.

"GRAN, GRAN, TELL THE ONE ABOUT THE HERRING vendors," says the little girl, snuggling up to her grandmother, "and how the fox plays dead in the road."

"And the vendors think they have a fine fox pelt," adds one boy.

"And they pick him up off the road and throw him

into their wagon!" says the other boy.

"And he eats the herring behind their backs," pipes the girl, "he eats and eats and then he takes more home to his family!"

"Well, now you have told it yourselves, haven't you?" says the old woman from under her covers, pretending to be offended.

"Oh, no, Gran, you tell it, you!"

And so she begins the story again.

Her voice lulls them all and soon their eyes begin to close, soon they are all asleep.

Only the old woman lies awake in the dark, listening to their breathing, the little girl curled up against her. And she lies there for a good long while, thinking once more of Merle in her tattered white shift with her long black hair, black as a blackbird's shiny wing, on the day the lord had brought her, saying, "Take care of this child, the nuns have done their best."

Her bones sleep now, somewhere in the riverbed.

"God have mercy on her soul," the old woman murmurs, and she crosses herself several times before closing her eyes.

A bear is breathing slowly under the earth, curled up in darkness under the snow-covered mountain. In a clearing above, a fox darts forward and his teeth snap around the neck of a rabbit. The taste of blood warm on his tongue and in his throat, the fox trots off with his prey, leaving red stains in the prints of his paws on the snow.

Farther down the mountain, the statues of the saints above the doors of the fortress chapel are covered with ice. Yet the colours of their eyes and cheeks can be seen through the armour that envelops them.

And farther still below, the abbot's mill wheel turns round and round, its paddles and spokes plunging into the icy winter river and the grinding of the stones mingling with the sound of the rushing waters. At the monastery, food is in short supply. One of the brothers has gone down into the cellar to fetch some dried apples and pears. Seizing the flat disks of dried fruit one by one, he drops them into the basket on his arm.

In February, the night is fourteen hours long, the day ten.

THE WAYSIDE INN IS FULL OF NOISE AND SMOKE from a fireplace that draws badly. All along the tables the travellers are dipping bread into their steaming bowls and talking and grumbling and laughing. A young soldier leans forward suddenly and pulls at the hand of another man seated across from him.

"Hey! You! Thomas! Are you not Thomas, the trobar? The fisherman's son?" The young fellow gets up and leaning across the board grips Thomas by both shoulders, shaking him roughly but affectionately.

"I know you!" the young soldier exclaims. "I have

seen you before. I was an apprentice to the lord Baudoin when you used to sing by the river mending your nets. We used to stop our horses and listen. What a voice! Tell me, is it true that Robert of Rochefort almost killed you for looking at his lady?"

And the young man laughs heartily but without a trace of malice.

Thomas listens quietly, dizzied by this chance encounter at a roadside inn, by this good-natured babble. Gaunt, bearded, he looks up into the innocent, enthusiastic eyes.

"Robert of Rochefort is dead now," says Thomas, and his voice rasps in his ears and reminds him of the hermit's voice. "And the lady Eloise has gone into the convent at Saugues after a long pilgrimage."

The young soldier stares at Thomas, his eyes darkening. Suddenly he speaks up again and reaching out, grasps Thomas by the arm.

"Look here, Thomas, why don't you come with us? We are for Jerusalem with Richard Lionheart! We could use a singer. Ship east with us. We could truly use a fellow like you! You could sing to make our hearts good and our spirits light."

Now Thomas is staring back at the soldier.

"What is your name?" he asks.

"Aimery." The young man smiles. "Nephew to the

lord Baudoin. Well, what do you say? Are you for Jerusalem?"

Thomas looks away. She is gone for him these many months. Yet he brings her back with the words and the music that he finds.

Again and again.

Clear fire out of the snow.

Sweet water from the salty sea.

He reaches for the young soldier's hand.

He reaches for the voyage.

THE AIR IS WARM, SWALLOWS SOAR AND WHEEL around the mountain fortress, uttering their piercing cries.

ON BOARD A SHIP BOUND FOR CYPRUS, THOMAS CAN no longer see the coast. All he sees moving above him and before him are the sky and the sea. Its sails full of wind, the ship heaves and rolls toward the east.

IN THE LORD BAUDOIN'S CASTLE, LITTLE JOHN IS running from the narrow window toward his grandmother's chair. Back and forth he runs, pulling a wooden horse on wheels. He is blond like his mother as a child but with Robert's dark eyes. He will be tall. Already his grandfather watches him in anticipation.

Baudoin prays that he will live long enough to see the boy on horseback.

JOHN DIPS HIS BRUSH INTO A BOWL OF DARK RED paint, the colour of oxblood. He is remembering the young man he killed. The little fellow's shoes had been torn and pieced together. He had had a mole on his upper lip. He had been light-boned, someone who should have gone to the priests had he had a decent life. But now John has wept for this human brother. He has knelt with Eloise and seen a thousand candles reflected in the paving stones of the basilica at Saint Jacques de Compostelle. He goes on with his painting, as he must. The dead boy lives in his hand.

ELOISE STANDS WITH THE OTHER WOMEN IN THE convent church. She closes her eyes. She sings with them and her singing rises with the chorus of voices and fills the space all around them and above them. She is free, she will not be given away again. A sparrow flutters down from the rafters and perches on the head of the sculpted wooden Virgin, ruffling its feathers. The Virgin's dress and hood are painted blue. Her cheeks are pink, her hair is yellow, her eyes are wide and dark and deep. On her knees, the child is sitting up straight, like a little man. The sparrow's chirping sounds in the midst of the singing.

FLORA CARRIES A BASKET OF WET CLOTHES UP FROM the river. In a bright room inside the convent she hangs them out to dry on a long pine pole that runs from wall to wall. Across a field, behind a line of trees, some people are dancing. The trembling notes of a bagpipe are carried on the wind. One two, one two, one two three four. Flora shakes out a wet dress and it makes a snapping sound, and then she hangs the dress over the pole and it begins to drip onto the floor. She picks up another wet bundle from the basket as she goes on listening to the music.

BABEL STANDS ON A PLATFORM IN A VILLAGE SQUARE. He begins to juggle, throwing his wooden sticks and balls into the air. A crowd has started to gather. Babel whistles and winks and begins to jump from side to side as he juggles. More people come. The boards tremble under his feet. Nearby, a chained bear is dancing, his mouth muzzled. His master jerks at the chain that runs through a ring in the bear's leather collar. The bear too is bobbing from side to side, a furry, fat clown with dull eyes. Babel jumps higher to keep the crowd's attention.

Matins, lauds, prime, terce, sext, none, vespers, compline.

In September, the night is twelve hours long, the day twelve.

ELOISE RECITES THE NAMES OF THE PLACES THAT John has told her about. Marseilles, Genoa, Rome, Messina, Rhodes, Paphos, Saint Jean d'Acre, Jaffa, Jerusalem … She opens a small casket and pulls out a gift from him, something he gave her after their pilgrimage, just before he went on his travels again. It is a glass vial containing water from the Jordan river and a palm leaf. She turns it around and around, watching the little bubble of air move from one end of the vial to the other.

BERNARD IS RUBBING A PUMICE STONE OVER A SHEET of vellum, making it as smooth as he can. First comes a scratching sound, then a softer buffing. The work is almost done.

BELOW THE FORTRESS THE BLACKSMITH'S HAMMER IS going at the forge, ringing beside the roaring fire and sending out showers of sparks all day long. Knives are being made, ploughshares and sickles, axes and axel trees, barrel hoops and arms for the new baron. Swords to be hammered straight, helmets knocked into shape again, resoldered, polished, sent back up the hill to the tower.

WHITE BONES LIE AT THE BOTTOM OF THE RIVER, rising and falling with the current as if they were breathing.

And all through the summer, in the mountain forest along a footpath where the peasant children go, faint laughter can be heard, and the liquid trilling of a blackbird.